SELKIE
IN
SEAL HARBOR

JEAN MARIE IVEY

Copyright © 2024 Jean Marie Ivey
All rights reserved
First Edition

PAGE PUBLISHING
Conneaut Lake, PA

First originally published by Page Publishing 2024

ISBN 979-8-89157-627-8 (pbk)
ISBN 979-8-89157-685-8 (digital)

Printed in the United States of America

CONTENTS

ACKNOWLEDGMENTS

My heartfelt thanks to all who helped make this selkie come to life in his human form. Special thanks to Jackie Davidson for her seal drawing that is cherished by people who live or visit Seal Harbor, Maine, and her aunt Margaret Wright, who told many stories about living in the village of Long Pond before it was moved to become the village of Seal Harbor.

Thank you to Paul Philipps, without whose encouragement I never would have told this story. He even endearingly learned to sing the selkie song.

Great appreciation to Ivey Menzietti and Donna Lee, my two oldest daughters, and other family members who listened and commented as this book progressed.

Thank you to Christopher Grindle and Peter Lindquist for the use of the book by George E. Street, *Mount Desert Island: A History*,[1] which was published at the very time that this story takes place. Chris found this very old copy that belonged to his grandfather when that book was first published back in 1905. When Chris and Peter found out I was writing a book about Seal Harbor at the turn of the century, Peter provided the complete book for me to use for my research. It proved invaluable.

Robert Rummel in Seal Harbor, Maine.
A signature of Christopher Grindle's grandfather in the 1905
copy of George E. Street's book that was used for my research.

---

[1] George E. Street, *Mount Desert: A History* (Cambridge: Houghton, Mifflin, and Company, Riverside Press, 1905).

JEAN MARIE IVEY

BOSTON AND NEW YORK
HOUGHTON, MIFFLIN AND COMPANY
The Riverside Press, Cambridge
1905

Much love went into the telling of this story.

SONG OF THE SELKIE

I am a selkie from the sea,
And on the land, a man I'll be.

I live beneath the waters.
I long to go ashore.
My love, she is awaiting.
It's she whom I adore.

I long for her and watch for her,
I know not why or where.
I have seen her bathing on the
beach,
Combing her golden hair.

I am a seal in the water,
Living far offshore,
On the ledges of Seal Harbor,
I watch the seagulls soar.

I want to glide among them,
Searching everywhere.
And to Poseidon, I offer
my passionate, fervent prayer.

I know someday I'll find her.
My heart, it tells me so.
And when I do, I'll marry her
And suffer no more woe.

I will seek to find my lover.
I know she's seeking me.
I am a lonely selkie
Living in the sea.

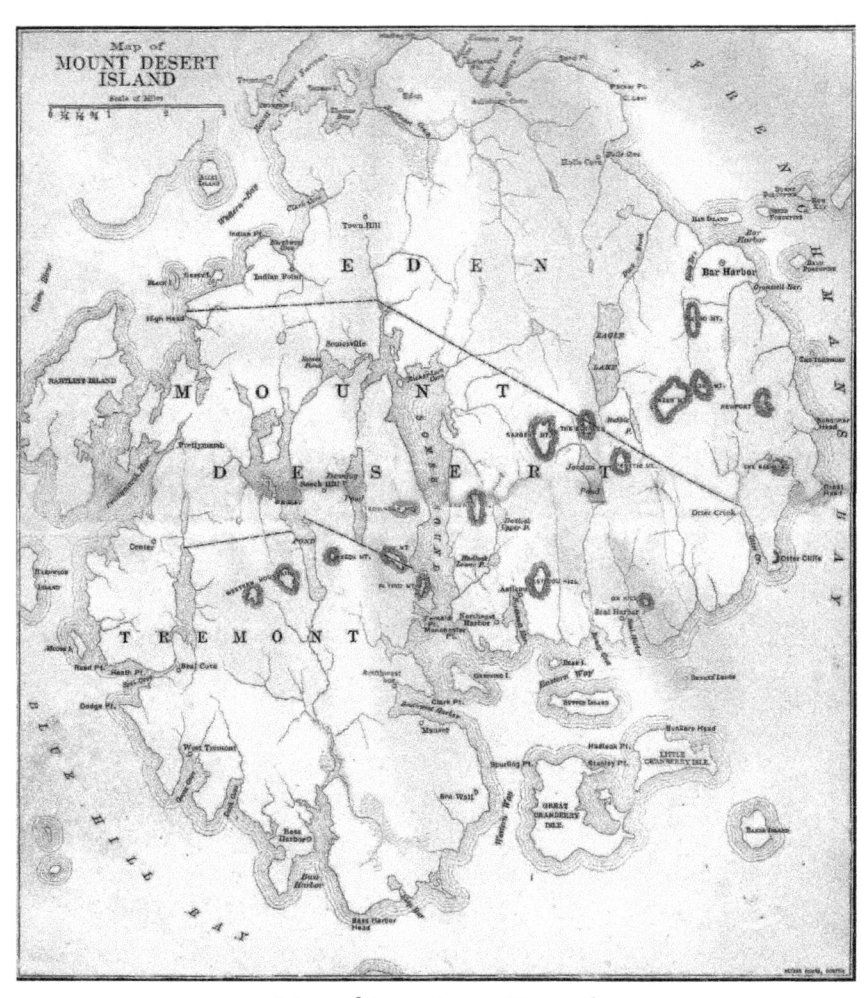

Map of Peter Engrs, Boston[2]

---

[2] George E. Street, *Mount Desert: A History* (Cambridge: Houghton, Mifflin, and Company, Riverside Press, 1905).

REÒLL

R is for *resourceful.*
E is for *eternal.*
O is for *omnipotent.*
L is for *loyal.*
L is for *love.*

Reòll was on a mission. Being a mythological being, an eternal, he remembered where he traveled from and what he was here to do. Remembering his journey to this planet was both a blessing and a curse. He remembered the Source—the brilliant white light, brighter than a thousand suns but not hot, filled with a universe of beings... all one. He was both connected to all and separate, an individual. He did not want to leave the Source but knew it was his calling, his time, and that he could and would return when his mission was accomplished.

He started as a spark, breaking away from his home and plummeting through the universe of universes toward this tiny blue planet that was inhabited by other beings precious to the Source. He chose this planet, knowing it would be difficult and painful, knowing that there would be love and suffering. He found himself in the crystal clear water off the coast of Maine, surrounded by his family of sea creatures, seals, and dolphins. Many of them came with him from the Source. His mission was clear—to protect a family that voyaged to America in 1851.

*****

In the 1840s, Reòll came to love a young girl named Catherine who lived near the coast of the North Sea in the most beautiful green land called Ireland. It was not a romantic love but a spiritual connection that came directly from the Source. She was filled with an unswerving faith in God and contagious optimism and was beloved by all.

3

Fighting the cold blustery waves, he would see her dancing on the beach to music coming from the picturesque house nestled into the side of a knoll with a sod roof where the family cow happily grazed.

Catherine loved to dance to music provided by her family and neighbors playing the bodhran made of goatskin, wooden beaters drumming, clacking bones and kitchen spoons, a penny whistle, and neighbors playing fiddles. They gathered frequently, and Catherine could not resist dancing a modified Irish jig, kicking up the sand, rocks, and seashells on the rocky shore.

Catherine appeared ethereal with the bluest eyes, the color of forget-me-nots. Little crinkles at the corners of her eyes were sculpted from laughter and smiles. Ivory coloring and dark-red hair swept back with ties kept it from falling into her face as she worked in the fields with her four brothers and two sisters.

This was the precious being that Reòll was sent to protect, knowing that her family would be going to America, and his mission was to keep them safe for future generations. He looked forward to that time when he would meet his true love in Maine.

Now Reòll was gratified to be a distant observer of the situation at hand. Catherine lived in a picturesque landscape with a long, winding road lined on each side by stone and wooden fences leading to an estate, not like the humble dwellings of the local people like Catherine's family and neighbors. There were horses and sheep grazing in the meadows surrounding the mansion. The scene belied the poverty and hard work necessary to maintain this existence. Catherine was not much more than a child and was tasked with being the breadwinner for the family as they were falling into poverty due to the oncoming famine and her father's inability to feed his family with farming. She was educated and well-liked by the lord of the estate, who hired her to tutor his children and do other household chores.

On her time away from her employment, Catherine came down to the sea to commune with nature. She somehow knew that there were friends awaiting her there.

Reòll sat on a rock nearby and watched as Catherine dipped her feet carefully in the pounding surf. He being an eternal and she a clairvoyant, they could communicate without words. He cautioned her to be careful in the water, and she thought about her life and her duties to the family. He guided her through thoughts for many years, and now was the time for the family to leave the farm and go to America.

It would take seven English pounds for each family member to secure the ticket. Catherine earned and saved enough money, and with her father's meager income from working in England during the famine, finally they had the fare to travel to the New World.

They went to Liverpool and boarded a full square-rigged, three-masted, gaffed sailing ship called *Manango*, which had made many transatlantic crossings carrying Irish immigrants to America. Reòll observed many of these crossings and knew that it would be rough, but that they would be safe. He felt her pain at leaving her beloved Ireland but knew it was her destiny.

In the days that followed, he and his cadre of seals and dolphins met the ship at the mouth of the Mersey River and followed the ship on its voyage. Sometimes, he saw the families dancing on the deck and heard Catherine singing with the little children, although he knew that the living conditions were harsh.

A terrible storm arose midway. The ship tossed. There was much seasickness. Reòll knew that there was not much that could be done, but he was assured by the Source that the ship would arrive safely in America, and it did.

THE VISION

Cassandra sat on the beach with her head resting on her knees, her arms wrapped around her legs. She wiggled her toes in the sand. She tried to weep but could not. Her heart was about to burst, and she prayed for God to end this sadness. *What is wrong with me?* she thought. *I am so full of grief and pain, and I don't know why.*

She had felt like this all spring. Pulling herself together when she was working, cleaning rooms at the inn, she always smiled at the guests and waited on their every need. Everyone loved her and thought she was delightful. But when she was alone, she fell into this unexplained depression.

Cassandra had always been a happy child, although misunderstood because she had a gift of sight. Often, it did not feel like a gift, feeling more like a curse. Now it was all she could do to get through a day. Lying in bed at night, she would repeat the Lord's Prayer repeatedly, praying for relief. But it seemed her prayers were not answered.

Her grandmother, Catherine, came to Maine many years ago to work for summer people. She died when Cassandra was young. Cassie was clairvoyant, and so was Catherine. So much so that Cassandra communed with her almost every day, especially now when she was so despondent.

God! What is happening to me?

She would eventually fall asleep and dream that she was drowning. Gasping for air, she would be startled awake. In the past, she had visions. At one time, she dreamed of a shipwreck, and she knew that people were in danger, but she did not know who or where or when. It took her all that summer, and with the help of Eddie Wind Eagle and his grandmother Blanche, her beloved Native friends, and her dearly loved dog, Foghorn; she solved the mystery. Her mother, named Mary, and her friend, Mae, from the lighthouse were saved from a watery grave. Foghorn was swept out to sea during the storm, and Cassie never forgave herself for his loss. Now it was she who was endangered, and try as she might, she could not fathom the source of her nightmares.

The wind and waves crashed. The sky was slate gray, almost black. She could see herself falling into the water. There was a child reaching out his arms with a silent scream. A vortex pulled her down, down, down. She could see a creature swimming, circling. She became entangled in the seaweed flowing back and forth with the waves near the bottom.

She awakened with a scream. Oh, how she hated that dream. People would hear her, and she would try to explain that it was a nightmare, and she would become so embarrassed.

Today was a gorgeous day. The sky was a shade of robin's-egg blue, the hue that looked like it was lit from within.

She raised her eyes and looked out to the sea and saw seals swimming offshore. Somehow, seeing those creatures gave her comfort. She saw gulls circling overhead and was sorry she had not brought table scraps from the inn to feed them. The ocean itself was a great comfort to her, knowing it cradled the ship that brought her family to America so long ago.

Now she needed to go back to work. She would visit Mae and Charles at the lighthouse soon, and she looked forward to that.

Dancing in the Moonlight

The night was warm with fireflies dancing on the breeze. Waves lapped the shallow shore, reflecting the full moon that graced the summer sky in all its splendor. A milky ribbon of stars kissed the horizon. Music from the inn drifted over a calm harbor, floating on a gentle breeze. A band was playing, and there were dancers on the porch spinning and twirling to "The Blue Danube" waltz. Beautiful women wearing long flowing dresses with upswept hair and men in their long-tail tuxedos were enjoying the summer evening with their riches and finery.

On the ledges outside the harbor, the seals were listening. On most evenings, they sounded like a barnyard, oinking and snorting at one another. But tonight, they were silent, listening to the melodies drifting toward them.

They slipped into the water and began the journey to the shore. There were fifty or so bobbing gently, as if hypnotized, toward land. The lead seal, slightly larger than the rest, arrived first. As he drifted onto the shore, he beckoned with his flippers for the others to follow, and they began to remove their skins and stand up, wiggling their toes in the wet sand.

There was the wreck of a sailing vessel on its side, washed up on the beach. It had been there for many years, and the masts were broken. A child's swing was attached to the main mast and swung to and fro as the boat rocked in the water at high tide. When the last selkie slipped out of its skin, the leader turned, raised his arms to the sky, and led the others to the ship where they hid their hides to keep them out of sight and safe from anyone who happened along.

Their human skin glistened in the moonlight. They were all so beautiful. The women and men had long, shiny hair. They found a part of the beach that was out of sight from the dirt road that separated the beach from the hillside upon which stood the Seaside Inn. And they began to dance. They were a mystical, magical assemblage. Some danced with each other, and some danced in rapture all alone with their faces lifted toward the full moon. One little girl who was smaller than the rest climbed into the swing, pumping her legs outstretched and dragging her toes through the seaweed and sand, kicking a sand dollar high into the air as she squealed with delight.

Cassandra left the inn as she did at about this time every night to walk on the beach. This night was no different. As she approached, she could see movement.

Oh, she thought, *there must be a herd of deer splashing in the water,* as they did most nights. On closer approach, she became aware that these were not animal creatures at all. These were the most beautiful human creatures that she had ever seen. She was a bit embarrassed because they were all naked, but she soon overcame that emotion because they were exquisite to look at.

She slipped into the woods and behind some very large rocks so as not to be seen. She sat down and was completely mesmerized at what was transforming before her.

There was one man taller than the rest. He was so handsome. She had an overwhelming desire to run to him but, of course, restrained her urges, knowing that any movement would send these creatures back into the water.

He looked startled for a moment, as if he heard a sound coming from the woods. It was like he sensed her presence. He turned and gazed in her direction, and she shrank behind her stone hiding place. She crouched down with her back against the rock for a moment and then couldn't resist peeking to see if he was still watching. He was not. Instead, he danced alone with outstretched arms leaning down and scooping a handful of wildflowers near the woods.

She longed to call out to him but resisted and watched while they retrieved their skins from the shipwreck. She was amazed to see them transform into seals once again, and they bobbed along the shore and into the water. She could see them swimming farther and farther out to sea as they disappeared, heading toward the ledges.

She sat there for a long time. The music had stopped, and all was quiet now. An owl swooped toward her and startled her out of her reverie. She found a path and slowly returned to the inn to ponder what she just experienced and to dream. For this moment, at least, she did not feel sad.

Going Home

Cassandra missed her family. She came to Seal Harbor in May, as she did for many summers, to work at the Seaside Inn in Seal Harbor. Learning the history of the island was one of her goals, and she learned that the first settler in Seal Harbor, in those days called Long Pond, about a hundred years ago, in 1809, was John Clement. He set up a bark tent until his log cabin could be built. He was a cooper and made barrels for the Hadlocks of Cranberry Isles. His sons were fishermen and caught smoked herring that they sold in the Boston market to accumulate enough money to buy the land where the Seaside Inn is now.

Over the years, the Clements made their home into a ten-room boardinghouse. A few years after that, the family redesigned the house into a large hotel and called it the Seaside Inn. It became a very popular resort for the rich and famous and an opportunity for local people to find work in the warm summer months. Cassie was amazed at the ingenuity and resourcefulness of the local people.

It was early in the season. She came to the island to help the Clements prepare for the summer season before the arrival of the Rusticators, as they were called.[3] She was very tired and really needed a few days off to visit her family.

On this day, she sat on the beach, chin in hands, elbows leaning on her knees, watching, and listening to the gentle waves. She thought of her grandmother Catherine and how she came to live in Maine.

Cassie was raised on a farm not far away on the mainland. She was used to hard work and loved people, so working as a housekeeper and server, where she could meet people from away, was a pleasant pastime for her and a means to help support her family. However, Seal Harbor was fairly isolated from the other towns on the

---

[3] The early "summer people" coming to Mount Desert from New York and Boston because their living conditions in Maine were rustic compared to their lifestyles back in the city.

island, and being on an island, it was challenging, time-consuming, and expensive to travel inland. Most visitors did not own their own boats and came by a combination of train and steamship. They could also take the train to Hancock Point, which was several miles north and on the other side of Frenchman's Bay, and then take a steamer to Eden. That still meant a long carriage ride to Seal Harbor. There was also a wooden toll bridge connecting the island to the mainland.

Automobiles were not permitted on Mount Desert Island. Traveling by carriage was too far and expensive, so Cassie was grateful for Jamie's boat and his willingness to come and get her to take her home. The town landing and steamboat wharf at the base of Ox Hill that rose four hundred feet from the harbor on the east was also the dock for the fishermen, local people, and recreational sailors.

Fortunately for Cassie, her young brother, James, had his own fishing boat and could fetch her to take her home when they both could find the time. He stayed with the Watson family in their home-town when their mom and Mae went to Boston on that fateful trip years ago.

Cassie smiled, remembering that even as a young boy, he loved being a lobster fisherman, knitting heads, mending traps, and paint-ing buoys.

He said, "Filling bait bags is really stinky, but it's a guy thing, and I love it."

Now he had his own boat and went out every morning at four o'clock and came off the water at about three in the afternoon, before dark, to unload his catch.

She frowned for a moment, thinking about the one thing that bothered him. He hated when the local fishermen killed the seals for stealing their bait. He loved the animals and was distressed to see them harmed. The thought of hurting the dolphins and seals broke her heart. It always bothered her to think of the whale oil used to keep the light burning in the lighthouse that she loved. She prayed for the day when there would be another way.

As she thought about the seals, she began remembering her grandmother, who reminisced about the animals, especially one seal that befriended her in Ireland. Catherine often talked about the seals and the dolphins that followed her to America, through terrible storms, and then reunited with her at the aquarium in Boston. Cassie thought that was an amazing story, but she was reluctant to talk about it because it sounded so strange. Mary, her mother, didn't believe in mystical tales and thought Catherine and Cassie were a little off, so to speak. Cassandra loved hearing about that special seal that befriended her family.

As she sat in the sand thinking about her grandmother's relationship with the animals, she glanced off to the right.

There was a very large seal sitting on the rocks near the woods. He stared at her intently. She caught his gaze and quickly looked away. Then she peeked back at him, and he was studying her. It looked like he was almost smiling.

Just then, several people from the inn came strolling along the beach, picking up sand dollars and sea urchins. They greeted Cassie, nodding and smiling. The seal saw them coming and slipped into the surf.

"Well! That was interesting," mused Cassie. Again she thought of her grandmother. "Even if it is uncomfortable, I will ask Mom to tell me about the animals and the aquarium in Boston before they moved to Maine. I know Mom has a diary that Grandmother kept of those times."

Now she couldn't think of anything other than those eyes. The eyes of the seal, as deep as the ocean.

JAMIE

Jamie was sailing to Seal Harbor in his pride and joy, his peapod. This was a gorgeous spring day in Maine. The sea was calm; the water cold. It was early in the season, and the lobster season was not yet in full swing, so he had the time to take a few hours to fetch his sister, Cassandra, to transport her to their home several miles Down East of Mount Desert Island.[4]

Growing up, she was his big sister and best friend. He was remembering when they worked and played in the barn together gathering eggs and taking care of Chestnut, the horse, and Brunhilde, the cow. They worked hard and played hard. He knew how fortunate he was to be raised in such a loving family. He and Cassie shared a sleeping loft in their cozy house that their father, Aaron, built out of the logs on the farm where they raised sheep and wonderful vegetables. He remembered the long carriage rides to church on Sundays with Aaron, who didn't attend the services, believing, like a lot of Maine men, that he could meet his spiritual needs on the ocean and in the woods. Mary, their mother, rode in the front, with the children and Foghorn their beloved dog in the back.

He was sad remembering Foghorn, who had been gone several years after he was swept out to sea in a horrible storm on that fateful day when Mary and Mae, the wife of the lighthouse keeper, were nearly lost. Foghorn saved their lives and the lives of all on that steamer. The light and siren were not working that day, and Foghorn, hating the tempest, snarled and howled loudly. The steamboat captain heard the barking and turned the ship away from the rocks and out to sea, claiming that barking dog saved them. As the storm raged, Foghorn was swept away, and Cassie never forgave herself.

That was several years ago, and today, Jamie had a surprise for her. Truly a miracle happened, and he could not wait to tell her.

---

[4] A nautical term referring to direction rather than location. When sailing from Boston, the prevailing winds along the coast of New England blew from the southwest, meaning ships sail downwind to go east (https://en.wikipedia.org/wiki/Down_East).

Jamie took up lobstering as a hobby and later a way of earning a living. He loved being on the water. He still helped his dad on the farm and sometimes helped Charles with the lighthouse, but fishing was what he wanted to do. When he graduated high school, he searched for just the right boat, and he found *Chickadee*, his peapod, at a nearby boatyard and purchased her with funds he saved for several years after falling in love with lobstering and enjoying the occupation.

His peapod was made of wood, a double ender that was easily rowed in either direction. It was built to be guided near shore from a standing position. It had a shallow draft and was easy to maneuver. Fifteen feet long, it got its name because it was like a peapod with the peas removed, sides spread wide apart held open by thwarts, with one seam down the middle. It was primarily propelled by oar. His boat also had a fairly large sail in the bow, which he was thankful for today because he had a long way to travel to get to Seal Harbor, and there was a gentle breeze. It was varnished wood with a red stipe around the top, and the sail was bright red. He named it *Chickadee*.

The town of Eastport, on the northeastern coast, several years ago built a lobster-canning industry. Lobstering at this time was a little scarce because of overfishing. A one-pound can of lobster meat sold for five cents, and it was a luxury in Boston. However, he was happy that he was not totally dependent on fishing for a living.

He was traveling south from a few miles north of the island and would soon be pulling up to the steamboat dock in Seal Harbor. As he approached, a school of dolphins swam by his boat, leaping out of the water and gliding gracefully by. He also saw a rather large handsome seal pop his head out of the water and watch him pull up to the wharf.

*****

Cassandra waited at the steamboat wharf in Seal Harbor. She sent a note to James that she would be waiting this afternoon for him and hoped he received the letter. She loved sitting and watching the comings and goings at the dock.

The wharf was long and wide to accommodate steamboats that were the main means of transportation off the island. The steamer *Islesford*, owned by Gilbert Hadlock of Little Cranberry Island, was moored at the dock this afternoon. A ramp on the right-hand side of the pier led steeply down to a lower dock that was used by fishermen and recreational boaters. It was surrounded by dinghies and rowboats. This is where Jamie would come alongside and gather her up. Also on the right side of the wharf near the front was a tall pair of davit cranes for lifting, pulling, and positioning heavy loads out of the water. Very near the crane was a rustic square building covered with shingles that had a large overhang where passengers could wait to board. Today the building was filled to capacity with beautifully-clad ladies and gentlemen awaiting boarding time on the *Islesford*.

The steamship had a large steam pipe. Tables and chairs were in the bow. Also there was seating in the stern of the boat. Large lifeboats on an upper level would be filled with passengers holding parasols aloft to protect from the scorching sun.

Cassie watched as the passengers boarded the boat and hoped that someday she could have a ride. She especially wanted to visit the Cranberry Isles and other towns on Mount Desert Island.

A little after two in the afternoon, Cassie could see Jamie's boat *Chickadee* rounding Ringing Point, named for the rhythmic clanging of the navigational buoy offshore. She jumped up and down, waving her arms with glee.

James maneuvered the *Chickadee* around the *Islesford* and up next to the fisherman's dock. Cassie caught the lines and helped secure the boat to the landing. She was good at tying knots, having spent so much time at the lighthouse near her home. James spanned the space between the boat and the dock with ease. He wrapped his arms around his sister, so happy to be with her. She had tears in her eyes, tears of joy, of course.

She took his hand and led him up the ramp to a bench on the dock and sat him down. Lunch in a picnic basket from the inn was ready. She had packed some leftover broiled chicken, fresh vegetables and popovers, and fresh butter and strawberry jam. James was hungry after his long journey, and he was happy for the meal. She also filled a jar full of lemonade made from freshly-squeezed lemons. When they were finished, there was some left that they could take with them. Their water trip up the coast would take several hours, and they could get thirsty.

It was getting late, and they needed to board the *Chickadee* and get under way. Cassie couldn't wait for a long weekend at home.

There was a nice breeze as they rowed out of the harbor.

Seals were waving their flippers on Seal Ledge, and Cassie waved back. When they cleared Ringing Point, Jamie set the sail, and they began tacking across Frenchman's Bay toward Hancock Point. The weather was perfect.

Cassie sat back in the boat and closed her eyes for a moment, savoring the warm breeze on her face. When she opened her eyes, she could see the town of Eden in the distance.[5] She was told by a visitor at the hotel that the word *Eden* meant "paradise," and she would not argue with that description as she gazed on the town with Green Mountain in the background. The first rays of the morning sun kissed the eastern coast of the United States as it dawned on

---

[5] The name Eden was changed to Bar Harbor in 1918, named after the sandbar that goes from the shore to Bar Island.

Green Mountain. She wished that she could see that, but Peppersass, the cog railway engine so named because the smokestack looked like a pepper-sauce bottle, no longer took passengers up the mountain.

As the island receded into a mist, she could see why the early explorers called it paradise. She was happy to spend the summer on Mount Desert Island. Now her thoughts turned to the farm and her family. As the peapod approached the mainland, they turned northward and sailed Down East. In a few hours, they would be home.

Cassie dozed off in the bow of the boat. Jamie was standing in the *Chickadee*, setting the sail, and guiding the tiller of the peapod toward the rocky cliffs of the shore.

As she opened her eyes, she could see the light shining across the water and hear the droning of the buoy and the sound of the siren at the base of the building. Her heart began to beat a little faster at the anticipation of seeing Mae and Charles and the cherished prisms of the sixteen-foot-tall Fresnel lens that was made up of many magnifying lenses and mirrors arranged in concentric circles and brass framework. It shimmered as it rotated around a lamp filled with whale oil.

The lighthouse was a forty-foot wooden structure, octagonal in shape. The keeper's house was painted white with wavy glass windows, polished clean by Mae, with window boxes full of lovely red flowers and bright-green ivy vines.

Jamie maneuvered the pod up next to a dock tied to a float held in place by floating buoys and anchored to the bottom of the inlet next to the cliff. There was a ladder attached to the escarpment where one could ascend from the float to the lighthouse, perched on the peninsula and surrounded by a yard with a vegetable garden that Mae tended all summer. The tide in this bay was very deep when high. Today it was about midtide when they arrived.

Cassie jumped onto the dock, and Jamie threw her a rope that she skillfully wrapped and secured around posts that would keep the *Chickadee* from floating away. When the boat was fixed, Cassie held tight to the ladder and climbed to the top.

Charles saw the boat coming and called to Mae, who ran out to the yard to greet Cassie and Jamie, who were like her own children. Mae and Charles did not have any other family and adored these two.

After many hugs and kisses, Cassie asked, "Where is Charles?"

"He is with the light. He doesn't rush to come down anymore since his accident several years ago."

"Well, I will go to him!" Cassie exclaimed as she scampered toward the building. "I can't wait to see him." She beamed.

Charles was waiting for her. He took her by the hand and guided her out to the porch-like walk outside the light. He picked her up and swung her around. She squealed with glee as he set her down, and she could gaze far out to sea. This was her favorite place in the world. Tears rolled down her cheeks as the wind blew her strawberry-blond hair across her face. She shivered a bit as the wind was always chilly up here. She could see the flashing multicolored lights, and there were dolphins and seals splashing and dancing in the water just offshore. This was truly her happy place. She thought about Foghorn and how she missed him, and she cried.

Charles and Cassie carefully climbed down the stairs of the lighthouse and into the kitchen, where Mae made a large pot of tea, and there was a plate of freshly-baked cookies.

She said, "You must be hungry and thirsty after your long journey. I don't want to keep you too long because I know your mother and Aaron are very anxious to see you. You have been away quite a while."

Cassie replied, "Yes, it has been a long time. The time passed quickly, and it has been very interesting learning about the island. It is very beautiful, and there are many visitors. I like taking care of them. It reminds me of Grandmother. She came to Maine with her wealthy Boston family to care for their summerhouse. She loved it so much that she decided to stay here with Mom. She never left after that. I will be glad to see my mother. I have many questions for her about when she lived in Boston during the war. Grandfather was away fighting, and she had a lot of time to spend alone with Mom. I know she spent time at an aquarium. It was the first aquarium for sea animals in the world. I hope she may have a journal or scrapbook or something like that. I have developed a fascination with the sea animals around Seal Harbor and have a lot of interest."

She and Jamie sat down at the table and helped themselves to the cookies. Charles had a sweet tooth, and Mae always spoiled him. It was her delight. She loved him so!

*****

Cassie and Jamie, their tummies full and warm, waved goodbye to Mae and Charles as they scampered along the pathway toward the road. Home was only a couple of miles away. Charles would have taken them in the buckboard, but Cassie wanted to savor every inch of the trail. She knew the way from many years of walking to the shore and back, where she could watch the great light. Jamie did too. Many a night he came to remind her to come home when she forgot the time.

Cassandra couldn't help but grab her brother's hand as they skipped along the cobblestone roadway. Like little kids, she remembered those evenings when they walked home together. Soon they were in the middle of their little village, hurrying past the church where they and their family attended services when they were growing up. They stopped in the general store for a candy treat to take to Mary, their mom, and then continued on their way.

There always seemed to be carriages clattering by as the two nimbly stepped to the side of the road.

"Hi, Cassie!" called out Mrs. Watson as she waved from her buggy on the way by.

Soon they came to the road leading to their house, which was perched on a slight rise. They could see the house surrounded by a white picket fence that kept the farm animals from eating the flowers and the kitchen garden planted off to the side, carefully cared for by Mary.

"Cassie, I told you I have a surprise for you!" exclaimed James as he gave her hand a little squeeze.

Just then, she could see a large animal bounding their way. At first, she was frightened. She stopped in her tracks and waited. As the animal got closer, she saw it looked like a big dog.

"Jamie, did Dad get a new farm animal to help with the sheep?"

"No, Cassie, just wait and see." He couldn't help but smile.

As the floppy-eared animal got closer, she squinted her eyes to see better.

"It looks like Foghorn, but it can't be!" she screamed as she fell to her knees.

The furry animal ran and leaped on her, licking her face, and barking uncontrollably. She threw her arms around the dog, and they rolled on the ground over and over as the tears streamed down her cheeks.

"How did this miracle happen?"

"I don't know, Cass. He just showed up at the door one day about a month ago. We were all so delighted. He seemed very thin and matted, like he had been living in the wild for a while. But somehow, he found his way home, and he seems so happy. Dad is grateful too because he really needed help with the flock. I guess we will never know what happened. He saved Mom and Mae, and now he is home. He will have to stay with Mom and Dad while you are away for the summer, but he will give you a reason to want to visit more often."

Foghorn was her best friend. She thought he was dead…gone, swept into the sea. He was a miracle to begin with. Charles had found him as a tiny puppy washed up between the rocks by the lighthouse during a terrible storm. Charles knew that Cassie was lonely, and it was almost her birthday, so with Mary's permission, he gave her the bundle of fur, and the two of them were never separated after that. Except, of course, when Foghorn helped Aaron with the farmwork. He proved to be depended upon by the whole family. He was so loved, and then he was gone as quickly as he came, swept out to sea in a gale…or so they thought.

The Surprise

The day was calm and beautiful, but Reòll sensed that a storm was brewing. He quickly swam toward the lighthouse where he often saw Charles tending the light. He rose to the surface and gazed off to the east where he could see a haze forming on the horizon. He knew that this could portend a coming gale.

Suddenly, the sea began to roll, and the wind blew harder, and the fog rolled in. Off in the distance, there was the sound of a foghorn, the kind that would be on a boat. *There must be a ship off to the south,* thought Reòll.

The rain began, and it was a microburst, cold and blustery. He looked ashore and noticed that the lighthouse beam was not shining, and the steam horn was not blasting the usual warning to ships and sailors passing by. Alarmed, he thought of Charles, who was always so conscientious to keep the lights burning when the sea was rough. He found a little inlet near some rocks offshore where he could wait and watch. Eventually, he heard a dog bark. He had not heard a sound like that before. This dog was like a foghorn. With each blast of lightning and thunder, he barked louder, like he was furious with the storm.

The steamship came closer, and it was apparent that it was blinded by the fog and out of control and was being drawn toward the rocks that surrounded the great light. As the boat approached, there was a huge gust of wind, and a woman's hat covered with ribbons and seagull feathers flew from the bow of the ship. A large eagle swooped down and swept up the hat and flew off in the rain. As the ship rolled ever closer to the shore, that dog ferociously barked. The ship's captain must have heard the dog and slowly turned the boat into the oncoming waves and began moving ever so slowly away from the shore and toward the raging sea.

Reòll thought, *That is one brave dog. He saved that ship.*

As the boat steered safely away from the coast, the barking stopped.

That's strange, thought Reòll as he swam away from his safe cove and toward the lighthouse. *That dog should still be barking because the lighthouse is still silent and dark. I want to make sure that dog is safe.*

As he came close to the rocks, he could see that the pooch was wedged between two of them and seemed to be holding on as best he could.

Oh dear, thought Reòll as he swam as close to the cliff as he possibly could. Suddenly, a large wave smashed into him, and the dog was swept into the ocean.

Reòll swam to him as quickly as he could. He dove under the dog, who grasped him by the neck and clung on for dear life. Reòll instantly recognized him as the little bundle of fur that he rescued several years ago. The little dog was swept off the stern of a passing boat, and Reòll saw him. The grateful pup scurried up on his back, and Reòll swam to the lighthouse and deposited him on the rocks as the storm raged. He knew that the lighthouse keeper would hear him and rescue him. And that is what happened. Now here he was again. He was a hero and had saved that ship and all aboard, and he deserved to live. So now he was clinging to Reòll once more. He seemed to recognize him and knew he was a friend.

The storm was subsiding. They had been swept quite a ways from the beacon, probably a few miles down the coast. Reòll wanted to make sure the storm was over before he deposited the dog on the beach. He knew that he would find his way back home, although it would take a while. Perhaps he would find a farmer or fisherman who would feed him until he was ready to look for his family.

For the second time in Foghorn's life, this kind creature had saved his life.

REÒLL'S LONG WAIT

Reòll and his cadre of sea creatures followed the *Manango* all the way from Liverpool, England. It was a rough crossing, but now the Clark family had arrived safely in America. As the ship rounded Cape May, entered a bay, and tacked slowly up the winding shallow river channel, it would take two more weeks to sail the final 110 miles to reach the port of Philadelphia. He could not follow her inland, so this would be when he and his sea family would say goodbye to Catherine and her family. It would be many years before they would meet again.

Being an eternal, time had no meaning to him. For Reòll, it would be but a few days, a few minutes. He had fulfilled his mission and watched over Catherine and her kin till they were safely in their new country.

In a few years, she would marry and, with her husband, Samuel, move to Boston near the ocean. They would have a large farm and raise horses and have a child that they named Mary. Catherine was very happy. Unfortunately, there was a terrible war among the states. Samuel went to fight, leaving Catherine to run the farm and raise their child. This was a suitable time for Reòll and Catherine to meet again. They needed each other. They were soulmates. But his true love that brought him to this world was not yet born. That was yet to come. Many earth years away and many missions were still to come. In the meantime, he was very concerned about two of his earthly siblings named Ned and Fanny.

Reòll and his herd swam up the coast and took up residence in Boston Harbor. Two of Reòll's favorite pups were a brother and sister. They were part of a smaller family, a bob of seals as they were referred to.[6] These two were especially friendly and intelligent, and he loved them. They were captured by a group of naturalists from the city. He was anxious to find out what became of them. For that, he would need help. He would wait patiently till they met again. He knew it would happen. It was destined to be.

---

[6]   Bob is another name for a herd of seals.

CASSANDRA AND MARY

Cassandra and Jamie continued walking toward the house hand in hand with Cassie holding on to the bandana tied around Foghorn's neck. She did not want to let him go. The tears were still streaming. She felt overcome.

Soon they came to the farmhouse. Mary was waiting on the porch with arms held out. She was still pretty, although she now had generous streaks of gray in her dark hair. She had a kind face with creamy, smooth skin. She didn't smile much. It was not her nature. However, she was smiling now. She was a loving mother.

Often lonely with her two children all grown and gone, she and Aaron spent as much time together as possible. He missed his kids too. He even went to church with Mary, though it wasn't his cup of tea, because he knew how much that meant to her. On Sunday mornings, they took the carriage with Chestnut and tied it up below the village green by the ocean until the religious service was over. Now Foghorn went with them in the carriage to keep Chestnut company while they were in church.

Cassie handed the bandana to Jamie so he could hold on to Foghorn, and she ran to her mother. Mary embraced her, and they spun around, not wanting to let go. Mary took Cassie's hand and led her into the kitchen that smelled so good, just as she remembered. Jamie followed with Foghorn. He was not offended that his mom made a bigger fuss over Cassie than she did over him. He was not gone so often and came regularly to help Aaron with the farm. He was glad that they were reunited.

Mary baked a cake and put a pot of water on the woodstove to heat for a cup of tea. Aaron would be in soon, and he and Jamie would want coffee.

Cassie talked and talked about the inn and the island and the town of Long Pond at Bracy Cove that was rapidly moving to Seal Harbor. "Mama, you must come and visit. You will love it there."

When they were finished with their dessert, they moved into the parlor with the afternoon sun streaming through the window and the smell of spring blossoms wafting on the breeze.

"Spring comes late in Maine, and everything blooms at once," exclaimed Cassie as she plunked herself down on the comfy couch. They talked for several hours about the farm and Foghorn and how hard Aaron worked every day.

"He's not getting any younger you know, Cassie, and neither am I."

The conversation began to wander toward what was first and foremost on Cassandra's mind. She was reluctant to bring the subject up because Mary never really understood Catherine and Cassie's clairvoyance, and it seemed to her to be paranormal and maybe a tad crazy. Mary believed that Foghorn saved the boatload of people, including Mae and her on that horrific day, but she could rationalize it by calling Foghorn's barking as his fear of the water.

Cassie knew better. He wouldn't have even been at the lighthouse that day if she had not had that vision that told her something terrible was about to happen. She knew without a doubt that Charles was in trouble and the great light was out and there was no siren. If it hadn't been for her visions, who knows what would have happened.

"Mama, I have made friends with the seals in Seal Harbor. I remember Grandmother talking about her seal friend in Ireland and at the aquarium in Boston. Did she talk to you about any of that, and do you remember going to the beach with her when you were little?"

Mary cupped her hand on her chin and said, "Hmmm, yes, I do remember going to the beach with Mom. It was very strange. We would sit on a rock and just watch the waves roll in. There was a seal that would swim ashore and sit a ways away from us. He—I think it was a he—would just sit there and look at Mama. Mama just sat and didn't say anything, and then sometimes she would say, 'Get back in the water now before you get caught.' I always thought that was strange.

"Mama took me to the aquarium in Boston. We always visited the seal hall. I remember that there were two adorable seals named

Ned and Fanny who did really phenomenal tricks. They were very popular with the audience."

"Mama, what else do you remember about those times?"

"Mama and I lived in Boston for several years. She maintained the horse farm for as long as she could. Those years when my dad, your grandpa, was away fighting in the war were really taxing and exhausting for her. She worked so hard to maintain the homestead. Because she was homesick for Ireland and the seashore, where she grew up and had a special seal friend, she took me, and we went on the long carriage ride to the beach several times a week. Mama always felt the ocean calling to her. It brought her peace.

"Your grandmother kept a journal of the years we lived in Massachusetts, especially regarding the aquarium. It is in the attic in a box back in the corner. I will see if I can find it, and we can read it together tomorrow.

"Now let's just think about what we would like for supper. You can go out and find your dad. He is with the flocks, and he will be so happy to see you. You go too, Jamie. This will be a happy suppertime tonight."

As she was preparing supper, Mary thought about the questions Cassie asked about her grandmother and the seal. It brought back memories of those days long ago. She remembered that first day that Catherine took her to the seashore. She was so excited to go.

*****

Boston 1861

It was a lovely day in the early spring, and the sky was robin's-egg blue with puffy white clouds. They found a long flat rock to sit on and watch the waves roll in. They fed the gulls with rolls left over from their breakfast. Other folks on the beach were also enjoying the warmth for so early in the year. She remembered how she wanted to hear news about her father from the letters that Catherine had in her pocket.

Her mother slowly opened the letters and began to read. It all was very depressing. That day, she paused and gazed off in the distance. Way off in the surf, she thought she could see a black ball bouncing in the water. As the ball got closer, she could see it was the head of a seal.

"Oh my goodness!" her mother exclaimed. "Mary, do you see that seal out in the water?"

"Yes, Mama, I do."

They watched as it came closer. After a few minutes, the seal slithered across the sand and came close to them on the shore. The animal just sat there looking at them, and Catherine appeared to recognize him.

Mary remembered her mother saying out loud to her, "His name is Reòll, and he is talking to me." She said he was sending her a stream of messages, which she began to understand. Catherine said out loud, shaking her head back and forth as if in amazement, "How can this be? How can this be, Reòll? Reòll! How did you get here from Ireland?"

Catherine turned toward Mary and said that the seal replied, "I followed you here. I have been waiting for you. Now there is something you can do for me. I have two little family members that I need help with. They were captured from our bob, and I am very worried. I have traced them to a building near the shore. It looks like a place where people can go to see sea animals. I am hoping you can find out what is going on there and if my siblings are okay."

Catherine replied out loud, "I am so happy to see you, Reòll. I missed you so much. I think I know the place where your kin were taken. I saw a poster tacked to a building that advertised a place where people could see sea animals in captivity for the first time. It is called an aquarium. I will see if I can find out what happened to them. If you were a person, I would hug you. But there are people coming, and you need to get off the beach. I will come by next week and tell you what I found out. Now get back in the water. I love you."

*****

That was some of what Mary remembered. She thought it was strange then, and she still was thinking it was unbelievable. She also remembered Catherine investigating what was called World's Museum, Menagerie, and Aquarium at 667 Washington Street in Boston.

Tomorrow, Mary thought, *I will look for that journal. It may have some answers to Cassie's questions.* Her curiosity was getting the best of her to try to tie those experiences that she was remembering to what Cassandra was dealing with now. *This is way too much for my mind to comprehend.* She shook it several times to clear the disbelief.

The next morning, Mary slipped past Cassie's bed in the loft as quietly as she could, being careful not to awaken her. There was a door in the back of the loft that led to the attic. She found a lantern and hung it on a hook in the rafters, removed the glass chimney, and lit the wick, carefully placing the chimney back on the lamp. She stood for a minute in the dusty head space in the center. There on the left was the big trunk that held all the memorabilia from her family, the letters from the war, and her mother's wedding dress. It filled her with nostalgia. Off in the corner was a large box that she hoped held her mother's journal.

She tiptoed over and ducked her head under the sloping eaves. She opened the box, and there it was—the journal. She carefully lifted it out of the container. The pages were fragile. She set it on the trunk so that she could extinguish the lantern, picked up the journal, and slipped out of the attic, past sleeping Cassie, and held the journal under her arm as she climbed down the ladder and into the kitchen where she set the journal on the kitchen table.

THE JOURNAL

After Cassandra had breakfast and the dishes were cleared, Mary sat down at the table. Cassie stretched her arms and yawned and opened Catherine's book. On the very first page was the poster advertising the new aquarium on Washington Street in Boston.

The poster she saw that she mentioned to Reòll said this:

Central Court…Washington Street
Inauguration
of the
Wonder Feat of the World.

Realization of the poet's dream and the
Age of fable brought into actual existence.
The whale harnessed to a
Shell-constructed car and
Driven around the
Mimic Sea
By a beautiful young lady of the city!
This astounding feat, which is unparalleled in the annals of
History, will take place
Every evening at eight o'clock and
Wednesday and Saturday afternoons at 3:00 p.m.
None should fail to see this novel and unprecedented
Illustration of the mythological Car of Venus.
The always increasing attractions of this splendid place of
Instruction and amusement, with the most complete aquarium
In the world, the finest and rarest collection of foreign
And domestic animals in the lower hall defy competition.

Performances at the usual hours, 11:00
a.m., 3:00 p.m., and 8:00 p.m.
Admittance $0.25. Children under ten years, $0.15.
Open from 9:00 a.m. till 10:00 p.m.[7]

Mary stated that Catherine found out that the original Aquarial Gardens in Boston was located on Washington Street in downtown Boston, adjacent to the Royal Gardens, and extended to the Boston Common and Granary Burying Grounds. It had high arched windows on the second and third floors that were designed for a large hall. This became the site for the first public aquarium in the world. It lays claim to being the first "pure" public aquarium in the world that was exclusively dedicated to the exhibition of marine life.

As Cassie and Mary began turning the brittle pages of Catherine's journal, Mary said, "Mama kept a journal for most of the ten years when we lived in Boston. This is the part of the record that she wrote after she reunited with Reòll. She updated him regularly about the aquarium and especially what she found out about his bob mates, Ned, and Fanny. They were the delight of their trainers and the Boston public, and she loved them too. This was the first entry in the journal."

*****

October 5, 1861

I took Mary to the aquarium, and I was fascinated with the main hall. There were forty tanks arranged in a circle filled with about thirty or forty gallons of water. The tanks were made of opaque glass. I found myself getting dizzy if I focused too long in any one spot. I asked an attendant how often the water in each tank was

---

[7] The Wonder Feat of the World is proclaimed in an ad from the *Boston Post* (December 26, 1861).

changed, and she said that it was never changed but had aerators designed to keep the water oxygenated. There were reservoirs filled with air that forced agitation that made the waters sweet. No plants were needed to clarify the water. Some rocks and sand and seaweed were arranged to appear as natural beaches but were not necessary in maintaining the water in the tanks.

"That was amazing to see."

There were all sort of crabs, starfish, sunfish, and sea anemones...

*****

Cassie thought as she read the journal that she had seen sea anemones on Mount Desert Island, and they were beautiful. They grew in tide pools around the island.

*****

There were more varieties of sea creatures than I care to mention in this challenge to my memory, but I will mention several more memorable exhibits. There was a menobranchus (fish lizard) from Lake Superior and a man-eating gray shark. "I'd like to know how they knew it ate a man." And next to the shark was a crocodile... yikes!

At the end of the hall, Mary and I looked into microscopes at a drop of water, sour yeast, a fly's eye, a spider's foot, and a diamond beetle. Mary did not like looking at that. I loved the music played by musicians and couldn't wait to get to the seal pool and other exhibits. Reòll especially wanted me to look in on the seals. He was worried about them and wanted to make sure they were okay. They were captured in July when they were three months old.

*****

I saw a catalog that no longer lists the menobranchus nor the gray and skate sharks. There were a number of different species of frogs and a dogfish. On the ground floor, there were new exhibits such as the introduction of a den of serpents with a South American boa constrictor and an African python. An opossum, pigeons from Penang, an agouti from Para, and a pelican from the Tortugas were also introduced.

There was also imported coral. I never saw coral before this, all colors...so lovely, and all kinds of fish and lobsters and scallops.

*****

Cassie laughed as she read, exclaiming, "I am no stranger to lobsters and scallops."

The journal continued:

In another catalog, a menobranchus reappears. A guinea pig, a Chinese monkey, a golden eagle, and a musk deer from Java have joined the collection. To judge by this catalog, it would appear that the mortality rate was not very high—but then again, most of the species exhibited were easily replaceable. Apparently, this enterprise is turning into more of a money-making scheme than a scientific pursuit. Makes me unhappy!

October 30, 1861

I finally got to see the seals that were now performing. Their names are Ned and Fanny, and the crowds that came to their shows loved them. They were trained by a man named James Cutting, who seemed to have a very special relationship with the animals and was able to elicit complicated deeds in a very short time. Ned played a hand organ. I was impressed when I read that James Cutting was truly interested in establishing a scientific endeavor and not necessarily in entertaining. Unfortunately, that was not what drove others that were more interested in making money. So unfortunate! Next year the newest aquarium called the Boston Aquarial and Zoological Gardens will open. I hope Ned and Fanny will be okay.

One of my favorite exhibits is the tautog (blackfish). It changes color to blend with its surroundings and comes to the top of the tank when called by a whistle or snap of the fingers. That was, to me, totally unexpected. The most beautiful animal I saw today, was as listed in the catalog, *Rhodactinia Davis* or most uncommonly known as a salmon-colored sea anemone, five inches in height with long tentacles, from the Antarctic. Many other animals, especially those that are easily replaced, appear in the new catalog.

November 1861

Now the aquarium has moved to a new and bigger location. I also heard that P. T. Barnum is now in charge. I hope he doesn't turn it into a circus. I read in the paper this morning that the

Atlantic Ocean is now flowing through the city of Boston because of the steam engines bringing salt water to the gardens direct from the harbor. Those engines pump six hundred thousand gallons a day into the tanks. That is such a ridiculous thing to say. People are so silly. There are many things that worry me about what is going on at the aquarium. I had such high hopes that it would be used only for good.

Oh my, Mr. Barnum is advertising something big is coming.

Now there was a whale in the center tank. My understanding is that it was sharing the tank with a dolphin and that it was twelve feet long and weighed twenty-one hundred pounds. That is heart-rending. It makes me want to cry. The whale did not live very long. How can anyone expect an animal like that to live in a little tank?

Summer 1862

I saw a catalog of the aquarium today and looked for Ned and Fanny. Fanny was not listed. She must have died in May or June. I will need to let Reòll know, although he probably already does. He has tried so diligently to see that those seals got what they needed. It was no wonder they learned their tricks so quickly with him working with them. He knew they would be treated with respect if they were bringing in customers. He has been so distressed at the treatment of the dolphins and whales.

August

Mary and I visited the aquarium again today. There are three whales there now. It seems like they are dying frequently. This is an abomination. P. T. Barnum opened another aquarial, zoological Garden in New York. He moves the whales from Boston to New York, but they always expire soon after arrival. I wish I knew how to make it stop.

Now the central tank is overcrowded with belugas. Barnum advertised that they will be moved to his new installation in New York. There were three living whales measuring nine, eleven, and twelve feet and weighing from eight hundred to one thousand pounds. This was the third pair that Barnum captured. The first two pairs did not survive. So sorrowful!

Under Barnum's ownership, the establishment was renamed the Barnum Aquarial Gardens. The description reads "museum of instruction and amusement." So much about this is disappointing and, to me, downright immoral. Barnum is much more interested in his New York establishment, and this one in the Boston Museum is going to be ruined. Now marine life is no longer featured. There is a black sea lion that weighs two thousand pounds and eats a hundred pounds of fish every day. It is the only sea lion that was ever captured alive. Barnum calls his new place of business the coolest place of amusement ever constructed. I say it was never meant to amuse but instead to educate. I am upset and not amused. Reòll will be devastated. How can he protect his friends and his herd from this greed and cruelty?

I read in the paper on December 1, 1862 that James Cutting was no longer with the institution. He was separated from the one living whale and Ned and all the other animals he loved and nurtured.

December 15, 1862

Now that Ned and Fanny are not alive and given the state of the institution, there is no longer any reason for Mary and me to follow the aquarium. I will tell Reòll that I need to say goodbye for the time being. My heart is broken. Samuel died at the Battle of Fredericksburg, and I have to settle up our estate. I need to find a job so that I can take care of Mary. I am beyond despair. What am I to do?

*****

Catherine moved with Mary to Maine in 1877.

*****

Cassandra and Mary remained at the table for a time in silence. Tears rolled down their cheeks as they remembered Catherine. She was adored by both. Mary didn't think she would recover from the grief when her mother died, and Cassie grieved but remained in spirit with her grandmother as they were both clairvoyant and always communicated in an intuitive sense. She was sad, of course, but always felt close and relied on her visions with Catherine when she needed advice.

Cassie arose and walked over to her mother. "Mama, thank you for sharing Grandmother's diary with me. I know it brought back memories for you that are mysterious and perhaps painful, but hearing this has helped me with understanding my own strange and mystical experiences. I hope that I have not made you feel uncomfortable. I love you very much. Thank you."

With that, Mary stood up and picked up the diary, held it close to her heart for a moment, and quietly backed away from Cassie without saying a word. She climbed the ladder to the loft and entered the attic to return the journal to its resting place in the box in the corner. As she closed the lid, she said a silent prayer for both her mother and Cassie and hoped that would be the end of the story. But she knew in her heart that it was only the beginning.

Cassandra walked toward the kitchen door, and as she opened it, she called to Mary, "Mama, I am going to visit Mae and Charles. I will be home for supper." She slipped out the door, stopping on the porch to admire the afternoon sun on the fields and the beautiful trees that separated the farm from the coast. Foghorn came bounding toward her, and she hugged him as she said, "Come on, Foghorn, let's go to the lighthouse."

Mae and Charles

Cassandra skipped through town feeling like she was a teenager again. Foghorn pranced beside her as if he knew their destination. Soon they came to the path through the woods that led to the road to the great light. Coming out of the woods, they could see the lighthouse with its beam beckoning to them. They began to run toward the keeper's house where they would find Mae baking cookies for Charles.

Mae was both Cassie's best friend and her confidant. She was the one person Cassie could come to who understood her and supported her and her mystical nature. She understood that Cassie's visions and Foghorn's relentless barking saved her and Mary's lives those years ago. Now she would listen and hope to understand what was on Cassie's mind today.

Mae was watching for them as they approached. She knew they would be coming because she saw the *Chickadee* moored below the rock face. She anticipated that they would go home first and would soon come to see them. She indeed baked cookies for both Charles and an extra batch for Cassie. Oh, how she loved that girl, now a woman, and couldn't wait to hear what she had conjured up since she moved away.

Mae called Charles, who was aloft with the beacon. He saw Cassie and Foghorn coming and descended slowly as he was still crippled from the day of the storm when he tripped, spilled the whale oil, slipped, and fell down the stairs of the tower. If it weren't for Cassie and Foghorn, he probably would have died, and the steamboat carrying Mae and Mary would have crashed on the rocks and broken apart. He really owed them their lives. He never forgave himself for the loss of Foghorn on that day and was overjoyed that he mysteriously returned.

Cassie knocked once, and the door opened, and Mae held her arms out, and Cassie fell into them with tears of joy at seeing her.

"Mae, you haven't changed a bit since I left. How are you and Charles doing?"

Charles was just coming through the kitchen door that led upstairs to the light and joined them in a group hug with Foghorn jumping and wagging his tail, happy to see his old friend.

Mae responded, "We are doing just fine. Come sit and have some tea and cookies while I look at you, then we can talk."

Charles enjoyed his delicious snack and couldn't get enough of ruffling Foghorn's fur. He couldn't believe his eyes when he saw him bounding through the door. He found that dog on the rocks outside the lighthouse when he was a tiny puppy and felt a special kinship and was heartbroken when he believed Foghorn was washed out to sea. Now he had to return to the light, but as he stood up to leave the kitchen, he turned to Cassie and said how much he appreciated Jamie's help in keeping the light and siren working smoothly. Cassie smiled as she rushed to hug Charles before he left the room.

She sat back down at the table and poured herself another cup of tea as she said, "I know you won't be surprised that I have some strange and unusual experiences to share with you, and I need your advice. There is no one else I feel that I can discuss these matters with, and I feel very lonely and sad."

Mae responded, "I am not at all surprised, and I cannot wait to hear what you have to share with me. I have missed you and your adventures since you moved to the town of Long Pond and Seal Harbor. Sweetheart, please tell me what's on your mind."

Cassie took another sip of hot tea and closed her eyes, letting the hot liquid soothe her throat, and she looked into Mae's loving eyes and began to speak.

"I don't know where to begin. Mae, you know I have always been a happy person. For the last few months, since I have been away, I have been in a veil of sadness, and I don't know why. It is like I am grieving for a person lost, and yet I know of no one except Grandmother who would make me feel that way. That does not make sense because I have always felt that she is close, and I can always speak to her. Also, when I sleep, even if it's just a nap, I have a vision of dying. I see myself in the water…wind howling and waves crashing. I am falling into the water with a child clinging to me, arms around my neck, screaming and pulling me down, down. There is a creature swimming around, circling, and then the dream ends. It is always the same. I am drowning, gasping for air, and then I scream and am startled awake, terrified! People hear me screaming, and I have to explain, and it is embarrassing. And then there are the seals."

Mae reached across the table and held Cassie's hand. She could see how sad and depressed she was and didn't know what to say. So she just said, "Go on! I can see by your eyes that there is more to tell. I remember how your vision of the steamboat came true and how you saved us. I'm certain that all will be revealed, and your faith will prevail."

Cassandra continued. "This part is really strange. Almost too strange for me to relate, but it is so real and intense. I somehow feel that it is related to my visions. I also feel that it is my destiny. I did not experience any of this until I moved to Seal Harbor.

"The telling of this, although I do not understand it at all, makes me incredibly happy. It takes away all the sadness and makes me want to sing and dance. There are seals in Seal Harbor. I see them sunning themselves on a ledge between the harbor and Cranberry Island. There are many of them. They seem to play with dolphins during the day. There is one special seal, larger than the rest, that I have seen in the water. I walk on the beach in the evening, sometimes after dark when my work at the inn is over for the day. One night, there was a full moon. The ocean was awash with light, and the water was calm, almost radiating light back to the heavens. Music drifted down the field, across the road to the beach. I found myself mesmerized as I walked along the shore. I looked out across the harbor and saw movement. As I waited, I could see heads bobbing and creatures swimming toward the shore. I was startled and quickly moved toward the rocks at the edge of the beach near the woods, and I found a place where I could watch without being seen.

"A large seal came upon the shore followed by many more. They were of all sizes and ages, even young ones, as it was early in the summer, and there were seal pups newly born. Then I watched as something unbelievable happened. The seals began to shed their skins, and they stood upright. They looked human as they tiptoed to a boat wreck on the shore where they hid their skins and found a place on the beach where they would not be seen by passersby. They were all so beautiful as they began to dance with the music from the hotel. They seemed so happy as they twirled with arms uplifted to the sky.

"One beautiful soul slipped away from the rest, seeming to look for something. He paused and smiled as if he heard me breathing. I was careful not to make a sound because I did not want to scare him away. I wanted so much to reach out to him. I was overcome with emotion. Soon he turned and danced away. The others began to don their skins and slip back into the water. The one special seal that I felt connected to was the last to be changed. I watched as they swam out of sight and most likely back to the ledges. I wanted so much to swim with them, but that, of course, was a ridiculous idea.

"From that time on, I cannot think of anything else. The sight of that man-seal never left my mind. He was like a song that repeated every time my mind was quiet. So now here I am sitting here, telling you an impossible scenario. The reason I came home was because I remembered Grandmother telling of a seal that she befriended when she was living in Boston during the war. I was hoping Mama would be able to remember what happened. It turned out that Grandmother kept a diary, and Mama and I read it together. It was an amazing story, and she shared it with me this morning. Now I don't know what to do or what will happen. I just know that I long for that seal to become human, and I want to be with him, Mae! What shall I do?"

Mae sat quietly for a moment, and then she spoke. "Cassie! You know there are many things in this world, in this life, that we do not understand. There are realities that God created that we cannot see. You have been given a gift that is not shared by many, and you must have faith that you will be guided along the way. I know because you saved me once, and I know that whatever happens is what is meant to be, and it will be good. I love you and am here for you whenever you need me. I hope to come and visit you in your new home sometime soon."

Cassie promised Mary that she would be home in time for supper, so she stood up and said, "It is time for me to go. I am so grateful to have you to talk to as these are not subjects that others would understand. I don't know who I will talk to when I return to the inn. Perhaps I can write you letters, and you can let me unburden myself. I don't know what I would do if I didn't have you. I love you so much."

She went to the tower door and called goodbye to Charles and then whispered, "Come on, Foghorn, it's time to go."

Foghorn had been sleeping under the table and bounded up, tail wagging. Cassie hugged Mae, and they stepped out into the evening air and began the walk back home.

SUNDAY MORNING

It was Sunday, and Cassie was delighted to attend her home church with Mary and Aaron. It was the village church that she attended with her family when she was growing up. The church was not like the new stone church she often attended in Seal Harbor. This church was small with white clapboard siding painted white. It was next to the village green that was across the road to the beach and the ocean, looking out to sea.

As she entered, the sunlight streamed through the stained-glass windows. They found a pew near the front where she remembered sitting as a child. She gazed out the windows and could see boats bouncing on the waves in the harbor.

She sat listening to the music and sang the hymns as the minister began to preach the sermon. She tried to concentrate, but her mind drifted to thinking about her grandmother's journal and the visit with Mae the day before. She also thought about her friend Eddie Wind Eagle, who helped her solve the mystery of the vision that saved her mother. He was there to help on that fateful day and later helped take care of the lighthouse duties while Charles recovered from his injuries. He along with Jamie continued to help Charles to this very day. Jamie helped during the winter when he wasn't fishing and Eddie during the summer months when his tribe was living at their summer village, and he was close by. Eddie was such a good friend. They spent a lot of time together at her secret spot on the beach where they could see the lighthouse and share visions.

The minister and accompanist knew Cassie would be attending this morning and arranged to play her favorite hymn. It was Catherine's favorite too.

> Brightly beams our Father's mercy,
> From His lighthouse evermore,
> But to us He gives the keeping
> Of the lights along the shore.
> Let the lower lights be burning!

Send a gleam across the wave!
Some poor struggling, fainting seaman
You may rescue; you may save.
Dark the night of sin has settled,
Loud the angry billows roar.
Eager eyes are watching, longing,
For the lights along the shore.
Trim your feeble lamp, my brother.
Some poor sailor, tempest-tossed,
Trying now to make the harbor,
In the darkness may be lost.[8]

She thought as the congregation sang that she would love to see Eddie again. She knew he often went to their secret place in the summer, and she thought, *I have one last day here. I will go to the beach on the chance that he might be there. He will likely be working at the lighthouse this afternoon, so perhaps he will be at the beach. I hope so.*

After church, the family returned home, and Cassie mentioned that she would like to spend a few hours at the shore.

Mary could see her melancholy and replied, "I think that is a splendid idea. I will pack you a lunch. You and Foghorn need a time to be together and reminisce."

---

[8] Philip P. Bliss, "Brightly Beams Our Father's Mercy" (1871).

EDDIE WIND EAGLE

Today is Sunday! My favorite day, thought Eddie because this was the day he could help Charles with the light. It was warm for late spring. The sun was shining, and there was an eagle circling overhead as he approached the special place along the shore. He knew that Cassie was visiting this weekend. He had not seen her since she moved away, and he missed his friend. They shared a special connection, not romantic as they were in their early teens, but still they were kindred spirits. He was pretty sure that being home, she would want to visit her favorite spot, hidden away from the rest of humanity.

"Oh, there is the rock where we had our picnics and watched Foghorn prance through the surf." He sat down on the rock and thought about his life since he last saw Cassie.

Eddie attended the University of Maine. It was originally called the Maine College of Agriculture and the Mechanic Arts and was changed just a few years ago to its present name. He wanted to be a spokesperson for his people and knew it was important to learn all he could about how to make things better for his tribe.

Early on, the Penobscot natives numbered in the thousands, but now there were only a little over three hundred living on Indian Island, his home. When Maine became a state in 1820, they were made to give up almost all their ancestral land and were left with only their village on what was to become the recognized Penobscot nation on Indian Island on the Penobscot River just a little north of Bangor.

He was passionate about baseball and played for the New England League. Eddie's hero was Louis Sockalexis, a member of his tribe who played baseball for the Cleveland Spiders. He was the first Native American to play on a major league baseball team, and some say he was the best player of all time. He was the grandson of the chief of the Bear clan. Once Eddie saw Louis hurl a baseball more than four hundred feet across the wide river to the far offshore. He was nicknamed the Deer Foot of the Diamond. Eddie loved Louis, who coached him and encouraged him to instruct the young boys on Indian Island. And that is what Eddie did.

Now Eddie walked along the hidden beach and hoped that his friend would be along. He found the boulder that they used to sit on and talk. Cassie was amazing; she instinctively knew his ancient language. He heard her singing once in a speech that he had not heard except by his elders, and he recognized it as from his heritage. She was chanting in a trancelike state and did not know what it meant. But he did. Now he would perch on their rock, watch the beacon from the lighthouse, and wait.

*****

Cassie and Foghorn strolled quickly through the village. She found the old path that she used to walk through to the shore. Being slightly overgrown, she took special care to step around the tree roots and over the baby firs that were growing in the path. As she approached the opening in the forest that led to the oceanfront, she could see the lighthouse. It brought back so many memories. As she stepped into the sunlight and looked down the beach, she could see a person sitting on her very large stone. She thought, *Who can that be? No one ever comes here.* She felt a little nervous.

As she approached, her heart leaped in her chest as she saw it was Eddie. "Oh my!" She began to run.

Eddie saw her coming and ran to her and swept her off her feet with a loving hug. "I thought I would find you here today, and here you are."

Hand in hand, they walked back to their special place and sat down on the rock. She offered him lunch. They talked for a while. He told her about his village and his people and his grandmother (Nokemes) Blanche, who helped her solve mysteries in the past, and she thanked him for taking care of Charles and how happy she was that he was friends with James.

Soon the conversation drifted to what was on her mind, and she told him about her sadness and the seals she saw dancing on the beach.

He knew about her mysticism and shared his knowledge of native medicine with her and helped her define her visions and was very interested in her otherworldly encounters.

Cassie drifted away in a bit of a trance, and Eddie whispered, "I brought my medicine pouch with me, and we can pray and have a blessing ceremony here on the shore."

He began preparing a place by the water. He shallowed out a spot in the wet sand near the tide line and gathered driftwood, lighting a small fire. Laying down blankets to sit upon, he beckoned her to join him by the embers. He chanted a melody in his native language, placed tobacco, sage, cedar, and sweet grass that he gathered in the marshes before she arrived, knowing that she would need his countenance, into a large clam shell, and lit them with a spark. Fanning the rising smoke with an eagle feather, as the smoke arose, he fanned it first upward toward the Creator, then speaking words of thanksgiving, he fanned the smoke toward Mother Earth, spiral-

ing the smoke toward the east and then toward the other three directions. Then he swept the eagle feather over the fire and over Cassie.

He looked up, and there was the eagle circling overhead as if to bless them. He closed his eyes and called upon Medowlinu, the powerful medicine people, the "little people." He looked toward Cassie and said, "I will ask the Mikum-wasus to help us, give us strength, and help find meaning in your visions."

Cassie slipped into a deeper trance. Everything began to spin. She should have felt dizzy, but she did not. Instead, she felt lifted to a higher plane of existence, perhaps another dimension. While in that place, she felt bliss and unconditional love. She saw the seals. She saw a beautiful man who appeared to be her husband, and she saw a child. She saw herself in a lovely place with a large and beautiful lake, and there were many people there. She seemed to be helping them, and they loved her. The clouds rolled in, and the place darkened almost like night. There was screaming and panic, and then there was sadness, unspeakable sadness.

She suddenly awakened, and she was weeping.

Eddie asked, "Whatever did you see?"

She answered, "Happiness beyond bounds and then grief beyond hope. Eddie, what does it mean?"

Eddie said, "I do not know what it means, but I can tell you some animal medicine that might help. Medicine that my people have taught me, especially about seals. That seems to be a source of your happiness. Let's focus on that. Let us pray together first."

They sat for a minute as the smoke arose from the fire. Eddie beckoned the smoke toward them to continue the blessing and began to tell about seal medicine.

"Seals represent active imagination, creativity, and lucid dreaming. We certainly know that represents you." He smiled, thinking of his friend.

"Seals are known as Pinnipedian, which means 'fin feet' or literally 'feather feet,' and they are more at home in the water than on the land. Seals will question your imagination and your balance. They want you to stay grounded and be careful who you listen to and who you follow. If seals are your totem, expect vivid and significant dreams."

They were quiet for a while.

Eddie then exclaimed, "Well! We certainly know that has come to pass, don't we? You must pay close attention and not dismiss as fantasy, no matter how unbelievable it sounds. Here are some things we know about seals. They come out of the water to rest and mate. They bear their young on land. This is significant as it shows the ability to bring and set into motion inner imagination and creativity, bringing these gifts from the inner to out in the open. It's what the world needs. This brings out the creative life force often associated with the faerie legends and ancient lore. That sounds really familiar, doesn't it? I think you need to pay attention to this revelation.

"Here is more that I am remembering about seals. This may surprise you that I have found this in my study of native medicine. I have heard stories told about water spirits that took the form of gray seals coming ashore, shedding their skins, and dancing in the moonlight, just as you saw them in Seal Harbor. I cannot explain this, but I wish I had been there with you to see that. It is said that these seals, turned human, are very beautiful. Human women who wish to have children can cry seven tears into the water and bring forth these beings as lovers from the depth of the ocean. There are no limits to the imagination of these creatures. You have been blessed to experience this phenomenon. What more can I say? I can't wait to hear what happens next."

Cassandra had long since awakened from her trance and was listening intently. "I don't know what to say. I do not know whether to be happy or sad, elated or scared. Eddie, thank you. You are a true kindred spirit, and I love you dearly. Thank you for everything you do for the people I love, and I hope we will see each other again soon."

Eddie sprinkled water on the fire to make sure it was completely out. The tide was coming in, so it would be washed away, and that was fitting as he hoped the blessing would be carried out to sea and maybe find a seal in its wake.

It was time to go. They embraced, and Eddie watched as Cassie vanished into the woods. He turned and ran down the beach toward the light, happy for his visit with his old friend.

MOUNT DESERT
𝔄 History
By GEORGE E. STREET

EDITED BY SAMUEL A. ELIOT
WITH A MEMORIAL INTRODUCTION BY
WILBERT L. ANDERSON

BOSTON AND NEW YORK
HOUGHTON, MIFFLIN AND COMPANY
The Riverside Press, Cambridge
1905

Cassie and the History of Mount Desert Island

Cassie loved her visit with family, was ecstatic with having Foghorn back, and appreciated more and more every day the beautiful surroundings of this part of Maine. She had never been out of the state, but hearing stories of other places and meeting people who came here from away, she began to realize that this place was very special.

Working at the Seaside Inn gave her an opportunity to talk to visitors who came here because of the beauty and lovely summer weather. Being intelligent and inquisitive, she endeared herself to many.

One sunny afternoon, she was outside sweeping the porch at the inn. It was the porch that overlooked Seal Harbor Beach. Usually the veranda was full of people fanning themselves as they chattered and snacked on ice cream and cookies. But today was different. The porch was empty except for an older man sitting alone with a book. He looked up and smiled at Cassandra, who stopped sweeping so as not to disturb him in his reading.

As she began to slip away, he spoke. "Hello, young lady. Do you live around here? I love this place. Some say that Seal Harbor is the most beautiful harbor in the world. What do you think?"

She replied, "I was born and raised on a farm a little north of here. I come to this place in the summer to help with the inn, and I am really happy here. There is so much I want to learn about this island. It is so unique, and even though very isolated, people found it and come from all over. The artists from New York come, and more and more visitors arrive every day. I have never been far from my home, and I want to know why people from other places find the island extraordinary."

He was enchanted by her beauty and curiosity but realized that she was a servant and not supposed to engage with the guests. "I have a friend who recently published this book about the island," he said, holding up the book called *Mount Desert Island: A History*. It was by George E. Street. "I am so sad that he died several years ago and never saw his book published. I just brought several copies to the inn because I think the people from away will be interested in knowing the history of this amazing island. If you have questions, Reverend Street is the person with the answers. Is there a time and place we could meet? We can talk about the history if you are interested."

She blushed, thinking she should not be talking with this person and also aware that he was a stranger. However, her curiosity got the best of her, and she replied, "My afternoon off is tomorrow. There are chairs on the green across from the beach. Perhaps if it is a nice day, we could meet there. I believe that would be appropriate. I really want to see this new book, and I have many questions I want to ask. Is that a suitable arrangement for you?"

He smiled broadly and said, "There is nothing I would like better than to discuss my friend's book. He was a man of the cloth, but history was his passion. It is his life's work. I will see you tomorrow after lunch if that is acceptable to you. I hope I haven't gotten you into hot water with this conversation."

"My goodness! I don't even know what that means. I will see you tomorrow."

Slow winging as the raven flies, the agelong past hath sped.

Still forests guard, the eagles wheel, the osprey soars overhead.

A thousand ghostlike snows, dream-white, when winter moons are keen,

A thousand drifts of bloom and song through tender mists of green.

The salmon's leap, the blue jay's flight, the shadowy canoe,

These are the memories of the years that ago and childhood knew.

And loves and hates have flared and died as council fires were blown,

Closed in the circle of the hills, unknowing and unknown!

Like sentinels, the moving tides, slow pacing to and fro,

Sweep to the ocean and return with strong and searching flow.

The olden sleep—the virgin peace—the song of life unsung,

All, as of yore, and guarded well as when the world was young!

Before the dawn float, fading mists, unveiling, as they die,

An empty sea whose blue waves leap beneath an empty sky,

An empty sea—save for a fleck of white upon the blue,

A lonely wing, of longer flight than ever seabird flew![9]

Cassie was so excited; she could hardly sleep. She wanted more than anything to be educated about her home, especially this island that everyone believed was so special.

She arose early and rushed through her chores, polishing silver, setting tables in the dining room, making sure there were candles on the tables on the porch for evening.

After lunch, she ran across the green to the awaiting chairs that overlooked the beach and the ocean. As she sat down, she glanced around and saw her new acquaintance

---

[9] From the poem read by Charles Campbell at the three hundredth anniversary of the landing of De Monts and Champlain at St. John, New Brunswick. From G. E. Street's book.

strolling toward her from the hotel. She could see he was carrying two copies of the book, and she anticipated that one was for her.

He sat down beside her, and they chatted for a moment about the view and the weather, and then he handed her the copy of his friend's book.

Cassie smiled and thanked him profusely as she turned the pages slowly.

He asked, "What are you particularly interested in, my dear?"

She replied, "Please, sir, tell me about Mr. Street and about why he wrote this."

*****

Cassie looked out to sea toward the seal's ledge and thought of all the wonders she experienced in her life on the Maine coast. She chuckled to herself, thinking, *I'll bet there isn't any history in that book that will explain that.* She smiled at her companion.

"My name is Henry Ingles. My friend, George Street, spent many summers in Southwest Harbor on the other side of Mount Desert Island. Do you know where that is?"

"Yes, I have never been there, but I heard tales of it."

"Dr. Street made friends with many locals and was eager to make the community better, so he founded the Southwest Harbor Village Improvement Society. He was dedicated to the morale and intellectual development of the area and its people. He was fascinated with local legends and enthusiastically tracked down the origins of truth and myth."

"Where was he educated?"

"He went to Yale, and in 1860, attended Andover Newton Theological Seminary. He was a very spiritual man. The war interrupted his religious pursuits, and he served in the Christian Commission at Potomac Creek and Fredericksburg, Virginia."

"Oh my goodness! My granddaddy died at the Battle of Fredericksburg. I wonder if they met." That made her very sad to think of Samuel O'Conner, her grandfather. She said, "If he had not been killed there, my grandmother and mom probably would not have moved to Maine." Fate and destiny fascinated her.

"After the war, George served a church in Wiscasset, Maine, just down the coast a bit. Then he moved to New Hampshire, where he served until he died. In the meantime, he, like so many, came to MDI each summer. This book is a testament to his love of this place. Now what would you like to talk about? We can meet again at another time so you can read more and know what questions you want to ask me."

"I guess my first question is, Who came here first? I know about the explorers, but who were the first settlers?"

"Let me read you some of what Dr. Street wrote:

> We make our history the record of merely material advance, and so the noise of axe and hammer drowns out the poetry. Is there not always more romance in brave endeavors that fail than in the equally brave endeavors that succeed. Shall we not do well to remind ourselves sometimes of the fortitude and zeal of the pioneers before the Pilgrims?[10]
>
> To the inquisitive and credulous minds of the men of the sixteenth century, the New World meant Eldorado.
>
> Gold mines reported by Indians are all the time referred to by early voyagers even on the New England shore.
>
> The sanguine prospectors believed everything they were told about the hidden wealth of the regions they had come to explore, and the shivering poverty of the naked Indians who were the only inhabitants of the newfound coasts did not undeceive them.[11]

---

[10] Saint Croix, G. E. Street.
[11] More from *Mount Desert Island: A History* by G. E. Street.

"In 1604, there was a colony of Jesuits from France that settled at Fernald Point on Somes Sound that was thought to be a river. That settlement did not last long. It was destroyed by the English who came from Jamestown, Virginia. There was constant strife between the French and English. There were Indians here then. Champlain saw them peering out from the headland, and the Jesuit company saw the fog rise, and when the hills came into view, there were Indians looking out and came alongside the ship in their canoes. According to the Jesuits, the proper name of the natives is Wabanaki, meaning 'the people of the place where the sky begins to look white in the morning' or 'the people of the east.' Champlain called the native people Etchemins, meaning 'people who live in canoes.'"

"Well, that is a silly name. I have a friend who is part of the Penobscot nation. I will love speaking to him about this. Eddie told me that the Indian name for this island was Pemetic, translated as 'that which is at the head' or 'sloping land.' That seems to make sense.

"Well, this has been a very interesting afternoon. Now I must get back to the inn for evening setups. Thank you very much for all the information and for this wonderful book. I will read as much as I can, and maybe if you come back to stay at the inn, we can meet again and talk. I want to learn as much as I can of the history of this island. Goodbye for now."

She scampered up the slope of the green and went back to work at the inn, getting ready for the evening meal.

TIME

Reòll awoke on Seal Ledge and watched the sunrise in the east over the Cranberry Islands. The beautiful pink light reminded him of the Source from whence he came. If it were not so lovely, he would have felt homesick. The time had come, in this three-dimensional world, to fulfill his mission, his destiny. In his timeless state of existence, he had been here for almost a century, awaiting union with his love, his mirror image, Cassandra. But how to bring it about? How to make it happen taxed his being, his imagination. He watched her come to the beach every day in the evening. She stood there gazing over the water, looking for him. He knew she longed for him also. He prayed hard to the Source of his being, "How can I make it happen? Thy will be done?"

He watched for Jamie to sail up the coast, and he would swim alongside the *Chickadee* and make little barking sounds to gain his attention. James would see him and gaze at him quizzically, not understanding. He was amazed that this seal was so tame, but he did not have Cassie's mystical ability to communicate.

Now it was time. Time to make it happen.

*****

Cassie walked down to the shore after she finished her duties each night. She remembered what Eddie told her about seal medicine. She did not particularly want children at present, so she was not about to weep seven tears in the ocean, but she did dream each night of that beautiful young man she saw dancing in the moonlight. How would she capture his skin to keep him human? Would he want to remain human? Night after night, she would fall into a depression, longing, and unable to know what to do.

On this night, she sat on what the locals called the time rock. It was a big flat boulder located near the woods on the right-hand side of the beach. It had verses about the passage of time inscribed in the top surface by some long-forgotten poet. It was a great place to sit and watch the boats in the harbor.

Tonight there was a full moon, and she could see seals swimming out in the harbor. The last time she saw them, the night they were dancing in the moonlight, they shed their skins and hid them in the boat wreck that was still on the beach. The tide was low, so the boat was well out of the water. Cassie remembered that the seals-turned-human were naked, and she was shy and did not want to confront a naked man, no matter how handsome he was. So she ran up the hill to the inn, hurried into the kitchen, grabbed a man's uniform, and put it into a basket. She left the inn and scurried down the hill to the shipwreck. She could see the seals getting closer as she went and hid in the wheel well of the boat, hoping that the seals would come and hide their skins in the vessel. She hoped she would be able to recognize her seal in the dark.

She waited patiently, being careful to hide out of sight. The music was playing at the inn, and she did not have long to wait. Soon the animals began coming ashore, one at a time. She could see out of a porthole her seal, and she watched as he peeled off his hide and stood, looking around as if looking for someone. He came aboard the boat and hid his skin underneath the main sail. Then he jumped over the side and, with the others, began to dance.

Cassie's heart began to beat faster and even hurt a bit; she was so overwhelmed. Quickly, she found his coat and replaced it with the uniform in the basket. She took the fur, held it close for a moment, and then found a place under the floorboards and hid it where she was sure he wouldn't find it. Then she waited, almost passing out in anticipation.

About an hour passed, and the seals, one by one came, donned their hides, and began flipping across the sand and into the water. Reòll was the last. He stood naked on the beach with his arms held high, looking at the moon as if to say, "Where is she?" He turned and looked toward the inn and stood for a moment, shaking his head back and forth and then staring at the sand. He climbed over the rail of the boat and looked under the sail for his coat. There he found the basket with the uniform.

He thought, *Can it be? Is this the night? Will my dreams come true?* He slipped into the clothing and leaped over the rim of the boat and stood in the moonlight and waited.

When Cassie saw this, she slipped out of her hiding place and stepped out of the wheel well. Reòll saw her and ran to the boat. He lifted her over the side and embraced her.

The world stopped spinning. There was a great light, like the aurora borealis only brighter and more colorful. It was like nothing either one had ever experienced. There was only love. Divine love. Love!

They stood in the moonlight embracing, unaware that the earth was moving and that their lives were changing forever. Reòll was completely human now, and his memory of the other world began to fade. For the first time, he began to be aware of the passage of time, and that was frightening. The stars were moving, and the ocean waves were crashing on the shore. He looked into Cassandra's eyes, searching for reassurance.

Cassandra was unaware of the changes that were overcoming her lover. She could feel the depression that possessed her for months lift and drift away in the gentle breeze.

He whispered in her ear, "I'm frightened. What are we going to do?"

Reality began to set in, and she held him a little closer. "I don't know yet. We need to think this over and have a plan. Come, let's sit and pray and talk about what we will do next. How are we going to explain this?" She wiped tears from her eyes and looked to the heavens.

She took his hand and led him to the time rock, where they sat very close because the evening air was quite chilly.

"I have hidden your fur coat so you cannot escape back into the water," she said with a giggle.

"Don't worry about that," he said. "I have waited my whole time on this earth for this moment to be with you, my beloved." He embraced her again. He felt safe in her arms and did not want to let her go.

"We need to find a place where you can stay. We will need a story as to how you came here. It will need to be both believable and true. You need a name. My family name is Wright. I think we can call you Bright because you are. You glow."

He seemed to be pleased with the name.

"Perhaps we can say I found you on the beach, and we do not know how you got here. That will certainly be the truth."

He smiled for the first time, and his face did light up. "I like the name, and my memory is beginning to fade. So what will we do next?"

"There is a winter, all-year-round church in the village of Long Pond and a brand-new stone church near the harbor. I believe we should find the minister. Hopefully he will be somewhere nearby. I hope he will want to help. Pastors are supposed to do that. There is a boardinghouse at Long Pond, and the pastor is usually there or sometimes a visiting minister. It is about a mile away. Do you think you can walk there? This is all so new to you."

"Yes, I can walk, but I will need you by my side because I do not know what to do."

"I will not leave you unless you tell me to."

Cassie and Reòll were thankful for the bright moonlight. They walked down the beach past a large natural hedge of wild rugosa roses. Off to the left, there was a bubbling brook flowing into the harbor.

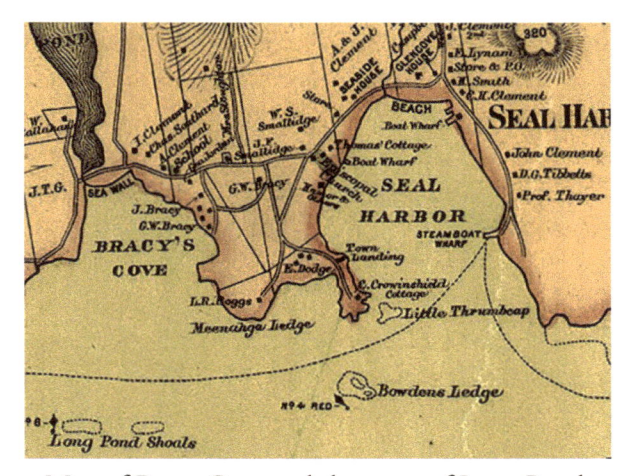

Map of Bracy Cove and the town of Long Pond.
Detail of George N. Colby map (1887) showing
the location of the hotels and stores.

They climbed up an embankment to the dirt road that separated the grounds to the Seaside House, and they began to walk
slowly so as not to draw attention. There were many visitors on the
inn's veranda. Soon they were beyond view, past the beach, and walking toward the village of Long Pond, walking up and over a steep hill
and down toward the town and the water on the other side. They
walked past the village store, the blacksmith house, and the school.

Cassie pointed out the neighboring houses. "These are people
you will get to know. They are good people, and when they hear your
story, I know they will want to help."

They turned onto another dirt road that went along Long Pond.
A short walk uphill led to the boardinghouse.

Cassie knocked on the door. A woman answered. Her name
was Anny Smith, and she recognized Cassandra and asked, "My dear,
whatever are you doing out here at night?"

Cassie replied, "Something unexplainable has happened. I
found this young man wandering on the beach. He seems to have
lost his memory. I went to the inn and got him some clothes to wear,
and I am looking for Pastor McDonald to see if we can provide him
with a place to stay and some assistance. Is the reverend here?"

"Yes! You are in luck. He arrived a few hours ago and is preparing for the Sunday service in the new stone church. Please wait here in the parlor, and I will ask him to come."

"Thank you. We really need help."

Soon Pastor McDonald came down the stairs and stood bewildered. Cassie spoke for Reòll and repeated the story that she told Mrs. Smith.

"What shall we do? I believe this man's name is Reòll Bright. He seems to have amnesia and cannot remember how he got here. Can you and the good church people help?"

Reverend McDonald looked at Anny and asked, "Can we put him up for a few days and see that he has food?"

"Yes! Of course, we can."

Cassie said, "I need to get back to the inn before they send out a search party. I am sure they are worried. I will check in first thing in the morning. I am so grateful that you are willing to care for Reòll." With that, she took Reòll's hands in hers, looked into his eyes, and exclaimed, "Reòll, this nice man and Mrs. Smith will take care of you tonight. I will be back in the morning to help decide what to do next. Are you going to be all right?"

He looked confused and a little scared, but he said, "Yes! I believe that God and these good people will look after me. I will see you in the morning. Thank you, sweet girl."

Jordan House at the village of Long Pond at Bracy's Cove.

Reverend McDonald was puzzled by the situation, not understanding the familiarity between Reòll and Cassie, but he knew Cassie and trusted her judgment. He was full of questions. "Cassie, you will need a ride back to the inn. It is late, and I will take you there. Please wait here while I get the carriage. Do you need something to drink before we leave?"

"No, thank you. I will appreciate a ride back though!"

Anny showed Reòll a room upstairs. Reòll had never seen or slept in a bed before and was puzzled. Anny could see his confusion. She remembered that Cassie said he had amnesia, and she imagined that he did not know what to do. Being a kind woman, she took his hand and led him to the bed, and she sat down and patted the covers, indicating that she wanted him to sit next to her, which he did. Then she stood up and pulled down the covers. She then went to a table standing by the wall that held a pitcher of water that she poured into a basin. She took a cloth and dipped it in the water. As she withdrew the cloth, she wrung out the excess water and dabbed the cloth on her face, indicating that Reòll should freshen up.

He smiled, nodding that he understood, and was amused at this use of water that he was quite familiar with.

She went to the bed and put her hands together beside her cheek, closing her eyes and tilting her head slightly to the right. She again patted the sheets, and he got the idea that she wanted him to climb into the bed to sleep. She told him that she would bring him something to eat, and she left the room, closing the door behind her.

Reòll was overwhelmed, but being omnipotent and an eternal, he knew that he would adapt and adjust. So he closed his eyes and sighed. He sat on the bed and smiled, knowing that he would see his love in the morning.

Anny soon returned with a bowl of fruit, a plate of goat cheese, and a glass of water, which she set on the table beside the bed. She also had with her a change of clothing, and with a broad smile, she slowly backed out through the door to the hallway, saying, "Good night."

Reòll did not quite know what to do with the food, but he was hungry. So he took a bite of an apple and a small piece of cheese. He then slipped out of his clothing and climbed into the bed to sleep. Tomorrow would be the beginning of the rest of his life.

*****

The inn was less than a mile away, but the reverend had time to ask questions of Cassie on the way.

"Where did you find this young man? This is all very strange. I would be very worried if I did not know you as well as I do."

"I was out for my evening walk on the beach." Not wanting to tell a lie, she formed her words carefully. "The moon was full and bright, and I sat on the time rock for a while and saw him by the boat on the beach. He looked confused and was stark naked. I know I should have been scared, but for some reason, I was not. I went to him and gave him my evening shawl to wrap around himself, and I asked him questions. It was apparent that he was not going to speak, so I set him down on the rock and pointed to the inn. Not knowing whether he would understand what I was saying, I explained that I would get him something to wear. He smiled as if he understood, so I ran up the hill to the inn and grabbed some waiter's clothing, returned, and he put them on. Then I explained that we needed to find him a place to go, and we walked to the boardinghouse. I thank you for helping him."

Reverend McDonald replied, "There is a doctor staying at the inn. We can ask if he will examine the young man to make sure he is okay, and tomorrow, we will tell the constable what happened and see if he can help us find out who Reòll is and where he came from."

"That will be the right thing to do. Thank you."

With that, they were arriving at the entrance to the inn. Cassie jumped out and thanked the reverend for all his help.

He smiled and said, "I will wait until you are safely inside before I leave. I look forward to seeing you in the morning."

"Yes! I will see you in the morning. Thank you again for all your assistance. Good night!" With that, she scampered into the servants' entrance to the inn.

REÒLL BECOMES HUMAN

After a sleepless night, tossing and turning and wondering what she should do next, Cassie awoke at dawn, leapt out of bed, and donned her uniform for the day's work. She went down to the kitchen where the cooks were preparing the morning breakfast for the guests. Everyone had already heard about the mystery man on the beach from the night before, and they greeted her with many questions. She provided answers as best she could and asked if she could be excused from her morning duties to go to Long Pond Boardinghouse to offer assistance.

The kitchen supervisor smiled and said, "Take as much time as you need, my dear, and keep us apprised of the details." He winked and made a little swishing motion with his hand.

She turned and bounded out of the door, down the steps, and ran down the path to the road. It didn't take long until Long Pond was in full view. In spite of all she had on her mind, she stopped, and the scene ahead of her took her breath away.

Oh, this is such a wonderful place to be. I hope Reòll and I can live here when we are together. She smiled and hurried along her way.

When she arrived, Reòll was already captivating everyone with his smile and ability to relate to people. Everything negative seemed to disappear. He had the ability to change the subject when asked questions that he could not answer without giving explanations about his origins or mission. Anny was serving him breakfast when Cassie entered the room. She giggled as she saw him looking at toast as if it were a piece of kelp. He drank a little juice, made a puckered-up face, and stared at the scrambled eggs. She sat down beside him and picked up his fork and took a bite. She was hungry and made like she was showing him how to eat it. Anny brought another knife and fork and set them in front of Cassie, and she proceeded to give him lessons on proper dining.

Soon Reverend McDonald arrived and took a seat at the table. Everyone was enchanted with Reòll. By the end of the morning, Reòll had won them all over, and Cassie was asking everyone for ideas on what he could do to make himself useful—until he regained his memory, of course.

Cassie needed to return to work before anyone became suspicious about her motives. So she left Reòll to fend for himself, and he was very good at that, not having a negative bone in his newly human body.

That evening, Cassie returned. Reòll was helping in the garden. Anny showed him how to pull weeds. He stopped every now and again to watch and listen to the birds. There were ducks on the pond, and he could talk to them, and they understood him. He went out of his way to make himself useful.

There was a little store nearby. He wandered in and asked if he could help stock shelves. It didn't take him long at all to find out what folks needed, and they, of course, were very happy at this busy time to have help.

Cassie found him in the dining room chatting with the guests, who thought he was charming. When she entered the room, he stood up, calmly walked over to her, and took her hands. "Thank you, young lady, for rescuing me last night on the beach. I am grateful." He winked at her and said, "I hope we can be friends."

She lowered her head so as not to show her smile and replied, "Of course."

They sat down together on a love seat and chatted quietly.

"It is hard to pretend that we do not know each other. We have been in love for a very long time. We will need to wait a little while, and then we will need to get married. You know that, don't you?"

"Married? What is that?" They still had the ability to communicate telepathically and could converse silently when necessary.

"Married means live together as man and woman. There are certain ways of doing things as humans to be socially acceptable. It will take a while for you to become accustomed to being human, but it will be worth it in the long run and make life a lot easier. You will need to trust me. I know it will be hard to wait."

"I have already waited a hundred years in your time. I can wait a little longer. I love you so much."

And so it was that Cassandra and Reòll began their life together, and they were beyond words to express their happiness.

REUNION

Cassie sent a postcard to James, telling him that he needed to come to get her for a weekend home.

> Please come on Friday. I have a surprise for Mama.

She hoped the message would get to him on time.

*****

James rounded Ringing Point and sailed into Seal Harbor. He could see Cassie sitting on a bench on the wharf. There was someone sitting beside her.

Who can that be that she is sitting with so closely, and with whom she is having such a serious conversation? His curiosity was piqued.

As he pulled up to the dock, Cassie and her companion bounded down the ramp, holding tightly to the rail as the sea was rocking the platform. James threw her a rope that she secured to the piling at the end of the pier. Her companion paid close attention, as if he was being given a lesson in boat docking.

James jumped onto the landing. Cassie embraced him and introduced him to Reòll without any explanation and invited her brother to follow her up the gangplank and sit down to feast on the luncheon she prepared from the inn.

The three of them seated themselves, and Cassie looked at Reòll and said, "Where do I start?"

Reòll spoke up and laughingly said, "I know you, James, even though you do not know me. You will find this hard to believe. I was the seal that accompanied your boat in the bay all those times when you visited Long Pond and Seal Harbor. I have been around for a very long time, waiting to be with Cassie, and now here I am."

James looked as if he was skeptical, but he was used to his sister's mystical visions and tales, so he tried not to show his incredulity.

"This lunch is delicious, Cassie, but we really need to get on our way. We have a long way to go. Please bring the rest of the food and drinks, and we can eat along the way. Let's go."

And with that, they climbed down the ramp, untied the *Chickadee*, and got under way. Reòll sat on the floor, giving Cassie the seat in the stern. Soon they were out in Frenchman's Bay sailing toward the mainland.

It did not take Reòll long to become friends with James. He was really good at that.

*****

Mae and Charles, who saw them coming, met them at the top of the ladder. There was much joy accompanied with hugs and kisses as Reòll stood by and watched with smiles. He was so happy to meet the person who had retrieved Foghorn as a puppy and saved him from the rocks where he had deposited him during that ferocious storm a long time ago.

Cassie explained that they did not have time to visit because they were anxious to get to the farm, but they would be back. Cassie introduced Reòll as her new friend and left it at that. More hugs were given, and they walked briskly down the path toward the village, waving as they went.

INTO THE WOODS

Every day was a learning experience for Reòll. Everything on land was new to him, and he was amazed and overwhelmed. As the three of them were plunged into the deep, dark woods, they walked slowly so that he could absorb the sights and sounds and smells.

He stopped to listen to the songbirds. "Oh, that sound is so beautiful. What is that?"

"That is a robin. See, it is sitting on the branch of the tree."

Reòll commented on the colors of the birds he saw. Cassie told him that the males were much more colorful than the females. He asked, "Why is that?"

She replied, "I think the males are colorful to attract a mate, and the girls are duller so they can be more easily protected and protect their young."

He responded, "That makes sense."

Reòll was familiar with seagulls and auk birds such as murres, guillemots, auklets, razorbills, and puffins. He also was friends with cormorants. They were his friends and companions in the water, but these creatures were so enchanting. He also watched raptors from his island and was not surprised when an eagle flew overhead. A red squirrel crossed their path, and Cassie laughed as he jumped back, startled. He spun around inquisitively, intensely studying each type of tree. He especially admired the fir trees because they smelled so good.

When they came out into the light and the village, he stepped aside as a horse-drawn carriage went by.

Old Friends

Soon they were on the dirt road leading to the farm. Hand in hand, they slowly approached the house. Reòll was taking it all in. He stopped to smell the wild roses along the road, and when they reached the house, he was captivated by Mary's flower garden. He wanted to smell each and every one. He turned and faced the pasture and asked all kinds of questions about the sheep. Cassie and James took him into the barn and introduced him to Brunhilde the cow and Chestnut the horse. He was a little nervous around the horse because of the size, but Cassie took his hand and showed him how to pet Chestnut's nuzzle, and he soon relaxed with the animals. He laughed at the chickens, and Cassie reached into the box and pulled out an egg and said, "We will have this for breakfast."

Reòll just shook his head.

Cassie said, "Let's go find Mama. She will be wondering where we are."

Just then, Foghorn saw Reòll. For the first time ever, he ran past Cassie and jumped on Reòll, barking and licking his face. He immediately recognized his friend and rescuer from the past, and Reòll was happy to see him too.

As they approached the house, Mary came out to the porch. "Who is this young man with you, Cassie?" There was something about him that looked familiar, but she could not tell what it was.

Aaron was behind Mary and reached out to shake Reòll's hand.

Reòll was not familiar with hand shaking but accepted Aaron's greeting, not wanting to offend. "This is all so new and strange. I hope I can make a good first impression," he whispered in Cassie's ear.

"You are doing just fine. Wait till Mama finds out who you are. She will be skeptical, so remember something that only you would know to convince her that you are her old friend from Boston." She looked at Mary and said, "Let's go in and sit down, and I will tell you all about my friend."

The kitchen smelled so good. Mary had fresh bread just out of the oven, and there was fresh fruit from the apple tree in the yard and a bowl of blueberries on the kitchen table. Mary offered them all a cup of tea, and after an awkward moment, Cassie said, "Mama. This is Reòll, your old friend the seal from Boston."

Mary shook her head in disbelief. She humored her daughter and believed that she and Foghorn saved her from a disaster years ago, but she still did not see or believe in her daughter's visions.

How was Cassie going to convince her mother that this was true and that her stories about the seals in Seal Harbor were authentic and that this really was Reòll?

She looked at him and said, "Talk to Mama. Tell her something that only you would know."

Reòll looked deeply into Mary's eyes and said, "Do you remember the birthday party that we had on the beach with your mother? It was your birthday. You had just come from visiting Fanny and Ned at the aquarium. You offered me a piece of birthday cake, which I refused, and you giggled. Remember how your mom and I could talk without speaking? She cried when your dad died in the war, and she wondered how she would take care of you. Do you remember how she wept when we parted, and you told me to go into the water quickly because there were people walking on the beach? Do you remember how I let you pet me, and you commented on my soft fur? I am Reòll! And I love your daughter. It is my mission and my destiny to be with her. I have waited a long time to become human, and I will be with her for all my time on this earth."

Mary began to weep. There was no way anyone could know these things unless they were there. "I believe you," she said as she walked around the table and hugged him.

Reòll also had tears in his eyes, glad to see his old friend again.

REÒLL AND THE LIGHT

It was Sunday morning. Cassie's family attended church, as usual, and introduced Reòll to their friends and the congregation. The introduction had no explanation other than Reòll and Cassie were engaged to be married and no details about the time or place where the event would occur. There were many questions, and most were averted by Reòll's charm and charisma. He had never been in a church before, and he was overcome with the sounds and smells. Of course, Cassie's favorite song was sung, and as the congregation sang, "Brightly beams our Father's mercy, from His lighthouse evermore," he imagined Charles keeping the light burning in what he thought of as a sacred place. It was where he deposited Foghorn many years ago and watched over it for years…waiting.

He had a beautiful voice but was not sure how to use it. Seals don't sing, but he wanted to. The sounds welled up inside, and he wanted the notes to come so he could join the melody.

"In time," Cassie whispered as she saw him struggle.

The smell of the flowers on the Communion table and the lighted candles drifted over him. The organ played sounds he only imagined. The drone of the minister's voice almost put him to sleep. He was so out of his realm.

Cassie put her head on his shoulder and patted his knee as the congregation began praying. He could feel the energy and closed his eyes, adjusting to another form of communication.

After the closing hymn and the greetings at the entrance, he was relieved to walk out into the sunlight and the familiar scent of the ocean breeze.

Arriving home and after lunch, Cassie stated that it was time to visit Mae and Charles. She said that she hoped Eddie would be there. "James, do you want to join us?"

"No! I need to help Dad with some chores. You run along and have a good time. I'll see you later."

They, Cassie and Reòll, walked slowly, stopping frequently to look at the landscape, admire a daisy or dandelion, or smell the aroma of the forest. When they came to the end of the path leading to the beach and the road to the lighthouse, they stopped and sat on a large piece of driftwood that was surrounded by sea lavender. Behind them and a little to the right was a bank of wild roses. The smells were exquisite. Again, Reòll wanted to sit for a while to take it all in.

Clouds began obscuring the sun, so they began the walk toward the lighthouse in case it started to rain. There was a blast from the siren, just in case.

Mae met them at the door and looked inquisitively at Reòll. She could see by the way he looked at Cassie that he was very special to her.

Reòll was taking in the smells of baking bread and cookies and listening to the sounds of the lighthouse.

Mae exclaimed, "Cassie! How are you, and who is this beautiful young man?"

"Mae! Let me start by saying my sadness is gone, and my seal has come home." She embraced Mae and giggled. "Mae, this is Reòll. He has come from the sea to be with me."

Mae's eyes were open wide, and she stared at Reòll. "Let me call Charles. He will have to hear all this." She walked to the door of the hallway that led to the stairs and the light and called, "Charles! Come down please. Cassie is here and wants to introduce you to her new beau."

Soon Charles burst through the door, grinning from ear to ear. "Let me meet this young man!" He rushed to greet Cassie with the usual bear hug and kiss on the forehead. As always, upon greeting her, he picked her up and swung her around and around as she laughed and hugged him back.

"Oh, Charles! I love you so."

Reòll stepped back and observed the greetings. He was amused and puzzled but glad to see Cassie so happy.

Cassie exclaimed, "This is Reòll! *He came out of the sea to be with me.* Oh!" Her voice was filled with glee. "That sounds like a song, doesn't it?"

Mae gestured for them to gather around the table. She poured the tea and brought forth the treats that were always waiting. Everyone talked at once, and then there was a moment of silence, and they began the stories.

Charles was speechless when Reòll related how he saved Foghorn as a puppy and how grateful he was that Charles rescued him from the crashing waves on that day so many years ago. Charles knew it was true because Reòll knew details that only a being who was there at the time would know. He was also thankful that Reòll rescued the dog again the day he, Charles, almost died falling down the circular stairs of the lighthouse during that visionary storm when the lights went out and Mae's steamship nearly crashed on the rocky shore. He was stunned to find out that Reòll was there, watching and waiting and helping in a way that only a being of the sea could.

They talked for several hours. At a point in the conversation, Reòll asked if he could visit the great light.

Charles chimed in, "Of course! Cassie, Eddie is tending the light. The three of you can visit, and you can show Reòll how everything works. I will take this opportunity to have another cookie and a cup of tea and visit with my sweet wife."

Cassie did not know that Eddie was there, and she was pleased to have him meet Reòll. She wondered how he would react to seeing his selkie vision in the flesh.

Cassie took Reòll by the arm and led him toward the spiral staircase leading up to the great light. As they climbed the stairs, Reòll began to feel his humanity. He thought as he climbed that experiencing emotions and the passage of time was becoming almost more than he could tolerate. He did not expect these feelings, having come from the timelessness of the Source. As a selkie seal, all he ever felt was love. He longed to be human with no understanding of what would be expected of him.

Cassie did not know what he was going through. He almost wished he could go back in the water or better yet go home. Of course, he looked at Cassandra and knew this was what he wanted, and he continued to ascend to the light.

When they reached the top, Cassie opened the door to the walkway, and they turned and entered the room where Eddie was tending the light.

He was so happy to see his friend but was a little confused at seeing Reòll. To be perfectly honest, he was a little jealous.

Cassie rushed to her friend and embraced him, saying, "Eddie, meet my selkie!" And she smiled.

Reòll succumbed to another human emotion. He too felt a little jealousy and didn't know what that meant.

Cassie explained that she and Eddie were friends for years. She said, "You know, being clairvoyant and having visions limits the number of friends and acquaintances one can have, and Eddie has been a valued mentor and kindred spirit, and I am grateful."

Reòll instantly recovered his composure and reached his hand out to Eddie, who accepted it with a grin.

"Well!" he exclaimed, "it is rare that I see my vision appear alive and right in front of me. Welcome to earth. Let me show you around." He introduced Reòll to the light as if it were a person and alive. "Light, meet Selkie. He has come to meet you and love and respect you as we do."

Reòll was mesmerized. He gazed at the prisms and lens and mirrors arranged in concentric circles encased in a brass framework. It shimmered as it rotated around a central lamp. Eddie began filling the lamp with liquid.

"What is that you are putting into the lamp?"

"This is what keeps the light burning. It is whale oil."

Reòll began feeling uncomfortable. "How do you get the whale oil?"

"Whalers catch the whale and extract the fat and melt it."

"Oh! Do they kill the whale?" He began feeling another emotion that was new. He felt anger. "That is so cruel."

"I know, but humankind needs the oil. We rely on it. And look how beautiful the light is. It is a life-giving circle. Sometimes we have to kill what we need to stay alive. Animals kill for food. Seals eat fish and birds. You must understand that."

"I am having a hard time contemplating that, but I know there are things I need to understand. Will you help me? Cassie has told me about your culture, and I know you understand these things and can guide me." He looked back at the light.

Eddie explained that they needed polishing every day to keep the prisms shiny as they gathered the beams and directed them twenty miles seaward. Eddie pointed toward the gears turning clockwise, powering the weights, suspended in the center of the tower, that turned the cogs. The prisms were rotating, spinning a myriad of colors that he hadn't seen since he came from the Source.

"It is a thing of beauty." His heart both hurt and rejoiced in the light's life-giving existence.

Cassie said, "I think that is enough for now." She led him back out to the walk around, and they stood at the rail. Seagulls were circling, and they were chattering at him. He understood what they were communicating, and it filled his heart with joy.

She looked out to sea. The sun was high in the sky and was reflecting like a million diamonds across the water. She said, "If you could see to the far shore, you could be in Ireland, where your journey began."

That took him by complete surprise, and his knees buckled at all the memories that swept over him. He said, "I need a few minutes alone to embrace what I am seeing and feeling. I hope you don't mind waiting for me downstairs."

"Of course, I don't mind." She kissed his cheek and carefully descended, holding tight to the railing on the stairs.

Reòll turned again to the ocean. The clouds that accompanied them on the way in had drifted away. He held fast to the railing. He was overcome with seeing the ocean from above when all he had ever experienced was the deep. He never knew what was above and beyond…that there was another world afar what he had known.

There is so much that we do not see when we are caught up in the world around us, as far as it goes, like a frog on a lily pad…imagine.

The sun was behind him and created a warm salmon-colored hue on the waves lapping against the rocks so far below. He thought about Ireland and Catherine and the voyage to America. He thought about all he was learning about being human.

"Human babies are born not knowing or remembering their source or what is their mission…why they are here. I was born a few days ago and need to acquire the knowledge that it takes a human baby twenty years to learn. If I had known what it would be like and how I would feel, I might not have volunteered for this mission."

As a selkie and an eternal all those years, all he felt was love and the yearning to become human. He wanted to experience human love, making love, having a family, but at what cost? He still felt the love unconditionally, but along with that emotion, he also felt fear, anger, a little lust, jealousy, and the hardest of all, the passage of time.

"It is hard being human."

THE DRESS

When Reòll and Cassie returned to the farm, there was still some daylight left with a pinkish glow on the horizon.

Cassie said, "Mama, while it is still light, I want to get Grandmother's wedding dress out of the attic. You know, Reòll and I will want to have a wedding soon. It is our destiny to be together. There is a new stone church in Seal Harbor. It is used mostly by the rusticators,[12] but I know Reverend McDonald, the pastor, and he knows Reòll too. I have so many friends and acquaintances in Long Pond and Seal Harbor, and since that is near where we met, it is where I want to have the ceremony. I take care of the children during church time, so I know we will be welcome even if we are locals. I hope you and Papa will understand. Of course, I want you to be there. You must come to Mount Desert Island soon anyway because it is one of the most beautiful places in the whole wide world. I can arrange for places to stay. It will be like a honeymoon, and we will not need to leave the island."

She scampered up the ladder to the second floor and opened the door to the large storage area. Lighting a lantern and carefully hanging it on a rafter, she carefully moved boxes and other treasures to uncover a large wooden storage chest. The chest was too heavy to lift, and it was back in the eaves where there was not enough headroom to stand, so she knelt and opened the trunk. She slowly began removing the contents. There were two boxes of letters, each tied with faded black ribbons. With sorrow, she remembered reading those letters written by her grandfather and Catherine's brothers, writing home from the War Between the States. There were also commemorative medals that they won during the conflict. She also found Celtic musical instruments her family brought with them from Ireland. There

---

[12] The people from New York and Boston coming to Mount Desert Island were called rusticators because their living conditions were rustic compared to their lifestyles back in the city. They built what they called cottages that were actually large mansions.

was a penny whistle, a small drum covered with goatskin embellished with faded Celtic symbols, and a pair of odd-looking strum sticks.

Setting these aside, she at last found the object of her search. Wrapped in brittle paper was her grandmother Catherine's wedding dress. She carefully set it aside and placed the other treasures back into the chest and closed the lid. With the dress in hand, she backed into the center of the attic where she could stand upright, removed the lantern from its peg, blew out the flame, and replaced it on the rafter.

As she left the attic, she lovingly held the dress to her heart, thinking of the day to come when she could wear it and walk down the aisle of the stone church at her own wedding. She knew Catherine would be there in spirit, celebrating the wedding of her beloved granddaughter and her selkie friend.

Reòll was in the fields with Aaron, James, and Foghorn, so he would not catch sight of the dress, honoring the old traditions. Mary took the dress from Cassie and held it up in the dimming evening light. The dress had aged from its ivory hue to a soft amber. The ribbon and lace were faded, but Mary thought they could easily be repaired or replaced. The pearl buttons holding together the neckline opening were all there. The dress was made of sheer organdy cloth from neck to shoulders, and the underskirt, yards of crinoline, was in good condition.

Mary exclaimed, "I can restore this. It will be beautiful." She was happy that Cassie would be getting married in her mother's dress, and she was glad that she could use her handiwork to make it lovely again. Something old, and the sash would be new. Now all that was needed was to find something blue. She began to be very excited about the coming event.

*****

Cassandra thought a lot about where the wedding would take place. When she first began working on Mount Desert Island, she was distressed that there were no churches available for the people who lived on the island year-round. The poverty of the settlers and the settlements on the island were so scattered, and there were difficulties of communication when the roads were nothing more than rough trails through the woods, and church organizations had a difficult beginning.

When Cassie first came to Long Pond and Seal Harbor, there were a few people meeting in the Long Pond schoolhouse. An occasional traveling minister might come for a funeral or wedding, but generally, there was no church. In 1901, a church with twelve members began meeting at the Seaside Inn, and Reverend Alexander McDonald, who lived in Seal Harbor, took charge. Soon after, a meetinghouse was built and dedicated, and at a public meeting, with a full and free discussion, it was voted unanimously to seek fellowship with the congregational denomination. That suited Cassie just fine as the little church in her village was that denomination. The meetinghouse with a congregation of twelve people was dedicated that summer, and that was Cassie's first summer working at the Seaside Inn on Mount Desert Island.

The congregation began to grow with the onslaught of summer visitors to the island each year. Cassie took care of the children during the services on Sunday, teaching them Bible stories and taking them for walks along the beach where they could collect sand dollars and sea-urchin shells. It was a happy time.

Cassie retrieved Reòll's fur hide from the boat where it was concealed, and she hid it in the overhang of the roof on the side of the balcony where the choir sat and sang, overlooking the congregation in the new church.[13] She was certain that no one would find it there. The myths and legends told  that if selkies who became human found their hides, they would slip them on and disappear back into the ocean. Reòll assured her that he had no intention of doing that, but she was not going to take any chances. So she hid the hide.

[13] Image of Seal Harbor Congregational Church adapted from a postcard (the Hugh C. Leighton Company, Portland, Maine, 1906).

Reòll's Sacrifice

To tell the truth, Reòll sacrificed his omnipotence and eternity to take on humanity. This was something he had not really contemplated in his time on this planet. He knew his mission and longed to be united in a human form with his love and mirror soul, Cassandra. He still retained his resourcefulness, loyalty, and most of all, his *love*. Now he had to live with his decision to move ahead in time and learn what it means to become a man.

He felt another unexpected emotion, and that was depression, about what he had given up. He wanted more than anything to unite with his love but came to the realization that union would take time. He also felt dependent on her, and that was an element of being that he hadn't experienced in the sea where he was king of his world. He did not like that needy feeling. Even though Cassie was full of love and longing herself, she couldn't help but be a bit controlling, knowing how new and strange this adventure was turning out to be.

Reòll did not like feeling resentful. He needed time on his own to explore. It was midseason, and Cassie was busy with her employment at the inn and all the other commitments she had with the children and the church and planning for their wedding. He needed to get away and gain some independence.

They sat on the beach and watched the ocean surf. Reòll could see his old friends the seals and dolphins leaping and playing in the swells. He felt a bit homesick. But that did not last long as he said, "Cassie, while you are working tomorrow, I am going to venture on the path through the woods to Jordan Pond. It is so beautiful. Maybe I can introduce myself to Mr. McIntire, and perhaps he could give me a job to do so I don't feel so useless. At present, you are supporting us both, and I want to help. Then at the end of the summer, when there is more time, we will get married and start our life together."

"Oh my! Do you think you will be okay without a guide?"

"Yes! You cannot take care of me forever. I am a man now and need to gain some self-respect. I know I have a lot to learn, so I need to dive in, so to speak. People here are so friendly, especially the locals. I will be fine. You have been so good to me. I want you to be proud of me. I love you so very much."

The path to Jordan Pond

Morning broke sunny and warm. Reòll was looking forward to his adventure. He had breakfast with Cassie very early, and then she led him to the Seaside path that led from the hotel directly to the Jordan Pond House about two miles away. She felt anxious letting him go off by himself, but she had faith that he would be able to take care of himself, and she knew if he met anyone, he would charm them, and they would help him along.

Oh my, what a lovely human he has turned out to be! she thought lovingly. She walked back to the inn, occasionally looking back until he disappeared into the woods.

He was enchanted by the sights and aromas along the well-groomed trail. He walked slowly at first, closing his eyes while he absorbed the aroma of the forest. He became aware of every fern and wildflower along the path. He heard a sound of breaking twigs off to the right. He stopped to listen and watched as a beautiful doe stepped onto the trail, followed by a yearling fawn, jumping and prancing around its mother. It still had spots on its back. The doe looked at the fawn as if to say, "For heaven's sake, stop cavorting."

She saw Reòll, was startled, stopped in her tracks, and stared at him. Her gaze met his, and their eyes locked.

He understood her and thought, *I have never seen a lovelier creature.* He nodded, and she and the little one quietly slipped into the thicket.

He studied the ferns and mushrooms along the path. It didn't take long until the trail opened up near the Pond House.[14] Reòll was  overcome with emotion at the beautiful vista that spread out before him. He became aware of little furry creatures scurrying through a field of goldenrod. There was an apple orchard on the grounds near the house and a field cleared of vegetation that sloped down to the pond, and off in the distance were two perfectly matched rounded mountains. The house was surrounded by soft, gentle lawns interspersed with flower beds throughout and surrounding the house. There were vegetable gardens used for meals. A stable, a carriage house, a woodshed, and an icehouse were on the east side of the main building and the road from Seal Harbor. Automobiles were not allowed on the island. Of course, Reòll had never seen a car and would not have understood how it moved noisily without legs.

Cassie spoke a lot to Reòll about the beauty of Jordan Pond, which was part of public reservation land. He didn't really know what that all meant, but he could tell that she loved it and wanted to be part of its preservation, whatever that meant, and she wanted him to realize why she loved it so much. He really didn't understand why it was endangered. He thought about the order of the ocean where

---

[14] Jordan Pond House inspired by a photo by Charles A. Townsend in *The Story of Jordan Pond House* (T. A. McIntire, 1915).

every creature had their space, as long as they had food. How could beings destroy their places of enjoyment and beauty or their food source?

He had so much to learn about human nature. Some things he just didn't like about humans, but he tried to be positive and think about things he could do to help. Certainly he did not want any of this landscape to change or be disrupted.

The reserve included all the mountains around the pond with a network of woodland paths that Cassie couldn't wait to explore when she wasn't so busy. These trails were said to be unequaled throughout the world. They would explore them together at the end of the summer.

*****

Cassie spoke of Mr. Thomas McIntire, who owned the Pond House and surrounding land, which was about sixty acres that was almost in the center of a mountain park called the reserve. Jordan Pond and all the surrounding area that included the Jordan Pond House was sought after by all who lived or visited the island. It was said that from all the towns on the island, all roads led to Jordan Pond. Mr. McIntire was an ardent hiker and a great lover of the outdoors, and he promoted the construction of trails on the island.

Cassandra spoke with guests at the inn who were dedicated to saving the unspoiled island, and she wanted to be involved. Next summer, she would volunteer to help.

She talked to Reòll about working with Mr. McIntire on the paths and trails after they were married and when they were settled. He was not sure what that all entailed but was willing to find out. He paused to absorb the spectacle that spread out in front of him, and it took his breath away.

Eddie Wind Eagle spoke to Cassie about the legend of how these two mountains got their name. The story was that there was a great battle between a good god and an evil god. The good god stood on Brassy Mountain, called such because of its golden color when the setting sun shone upon it. The evil god stood on Pemetic Mountain. A great battle ensued, and the good god fell from his mountain and into Jordan Pond. On his way down, he pulled away two mounds of the cliff rocks that buried the evil god forever. The falling rocks became the two mountains overlooking the pond. That victory of the good god brought peace and good fortune to the valley. The two mountains were also referred to by the natives as the female anatomy that they resemble. Of course, Reòll was naive and didn't understand any of that.

Now here he was gazing at the vista and wondering what he should do next. He walked into the front door of the Pond House.

Cassie Learning the History of Seal Harbor

Cassie was always full of questions. Coming from a farm and a much simpler life, she wanted to know about this wonderful place that she was adopting for her new home.

She met several wealthy people who stayed at the Seaside Inn and also spoke to others who stayed at the Glen Cove Hotel just a short distance from the Seaside and directly across from the beach in Seal Harbor. That hotel was not very attractive, and a lot of people were annoyed at its presence. The Seaside Inn was higher up the hill and closer to the village of Long Pond. Glen Cove was nearer to the main part of town. It consisted of two square wooden buildings connected across a deep ravine with a brook at the bottom by a long high bridge. It was referred to by many as the Hyphen.

Always interested in history and knowledge, Cassie was impressed with the intellectual guests who stayed there, such as scientists and college professors. She always wanted to learn new things. Cassie thought it was funny that the bell boys sometimes spoke Latin prose with the guests.[15]

One day, she was sitting on the beach sunning herself when she was approached by a portly man who looked to be maybe in his early thirties. He nodded and stated, "This is one of the most beautiful places I have ever visited. Do you live around here?"

She replied, "Yes! My home is Down East, which just means up the coast." She smiled. "I work at the Seaside Inn in the summer. I love it here. Hope to be married soon and become a permanent resident. Where are you from? From your British accent, I believe you are not from here."

"No!" he replied with a swishing hand gesture as if he was about to give a speech. "I was elected to the British Parliament a few years

---

[15] Some of this information about the early history of Seal Harbor and Winston Churchill came from random notes of George L. Stebbins.

ago, but what I love most is writing. I am inspired by this place. My name is Winston Churchill. I am only here for a few days staying at the Glen Cove, and then I will return to England." He thanked her for her friendly demeanor and walked back toward the hotel that was across the road from the beach.

Cassie was impressed by his charisma and stature and his way of speaking. She thought, *This man has a future in politics. He could charm the dessert right off the table no matter how sweet it was. And I'll bet he would like that too.* Smiling at the thought, she wished she could get to know him better.

In earlier days, there was no road access to the shorefront until it was opened up by Mr. and Mrs. George Cooksey, who were wealthy summer residents, when they built a cottage in 1894 on the point of the east side of the harbor. Later, Mr. Cooksey bought eight hundred acres from the shorefront to Little Hunter's Beach. Drs. Edward K. Dunham and Christian A. Herter built well-equipped laboratories on the point that, with regular testing, ensured clean milk and water to the area.

Cassie heard a story about the monkeys at the laboratories that were used for research into spinal meningitis. One of the guests at the hotel told her a story. He related that Dr. Herter was doing experiments, and one day, a cage door was left open, and the monkeys escaped into the woods. A cook for a summer resident in a nearby cottage was cooking a steak for the noonday meal and nipping a bit of the cup that cheers. The steak smelled really good, and the kitchen window was open. A monkey jumped through it and onto the cook's shoulder. Imagine her surprise as she screamed and ran to the master of the house, startled himself, as he drove out the animal.

Cassie laughed and also felt sorry for the cook, thinking of how terrified she must have been.

Cassie was curious about how the town received the beautiful clean water, pure and unspoiled from Jordan Pond. It tasted so sweet. Most of her information came from guests, but this came from one of her colleagues who lived in the village of Long Pond most of his life. His name was Ion Smallidge, and he was a local. He lived in a house on the right side of the road between Seal Harbor and Bracy

Cove. He said, "In the early 1900s, there were only a few summer cottages and houses of local residents. Most were in the village of Long Pond. When the summer visitors built their cottages, mostly on Ox Hill, they realized that they needed a water supply and that it would have to be supplied by Jordan Pond, two miles away. It had to come from the outlet of the pond, down the Jordan Brook to the foot of Long Pond. Pipe was ordered, and it took all the available pipe in Boston shipped to Mount Desert Ferry and a steamboat with Captain William Cox of Seal Harbor on board to transport it. When the schooner arrived off Cooksey's Point, called Reef Point at the time, Mr. Cooksey, wishing to help, went out on the point and shouted. Captain Cox, wishing to hear the waves on the rocks and not recognizing the voice, shouted back, 'Shut up, you damned fool!'"

Cassie mused, "He must have been really embarrassed when he found out who he had insulted."

The water coming from Jordan Pond to the village created rapid growth along the Jordan Pond Road. Many locals moved there, moving their houses from Long Pond.

Now she wanted to know more about the McIntires and the Jordan Pond House. She thought a lot about what she and Reòll would do and where they would live after they were married.

REÒLL MEETS MR. THOMAS MCINTIRE

Reòll stood in the entrance to the Jordan Pond House. He was met by someone who appeared to be looking after the guests. She was a lovely young woman who had a name tag from a college he did not recognize, and she spoke to him so kindly.

"Can I help you, sir? Are you here for tea?"

Reòll replied, "Thank you for your assistance. I am here to see Mr. McIntire."

"He is very busy at the moment overseeing the dining room. Can you tell me why you are here, and I will go find him?"

Reòll said, "I am the intended of Cassandra Wright, and I am here to see if Mr. McIntire can find me employment. I would appreciate it if you could tell him I'm here."

"Certainly, sir! I will go now."

It was obvious that she recognized Cassie's name. Reòll smiled, thinking, *Everyone knows her. She is so smart and friendly. I love her so much.*

Very soon, a stately-looking gentleman sauntered out of the kitchen. He was tall and had a little mustache and a very large smile. "So you are engaged to marry Cassie? You are a very lucky man," he said, thrusting his hand forward.

Reòll was beginning to feel comfortable with this male form of greeting, and he accepted the handshake gladly, pressing his other hand over Mr. Thomas's in a friendly manner. "Yes!" he exclaimed. "She is working at the inn, supporting us both, and I am very anxious to find employment. She suggested that I come to you because she admires what you are doing here. We both want to help with your preservation plans and the building of the paths. You probably know my story, how I arrived with no explanation and amnesia. I don't know what I can do, but I am a fast learner, friendly, and willing. I will appreciate anything you can offer."

Mr. McIntire looked quizzically into Reòll's eyes and saw something special. He didn't know what it was about him, but he knew he liked what he saw. He said, "You know, I was just looking for a new gardener. I have a very large vegetable garden and lots of flowers that need tending. I'll bet that would be right up your road, so to speak. Can you start tomorrow?"

"That would be so good. I love gardening. I have been helping out in the village with flowers for the cottages. Yes! I will start tomorrow. Cassie will be so delighted. Thank you. I am amazed at this place. I didn't know anything on this earth could be so beautiful."

With that, he shook hands again and walked out into the sunlight. He began walking past the front lawn where there were rustic wooden tables and chairs in the shade of birch trees.

As he approached the pond, quite a ways down the sloping fields, clouds began forming overhead. He hoped it wouldn't rain because he had a long way to walk home. Then he thought, *That's silly! Why would I let a little water bother me?* And he giggled.

There was an older woman sitting on a large rock about nine hundred feet on the east shore of the pond. He walked along slowly, allowing the beauty of the scene before him to wash over his consciousness and fill him with joy. He approached the woman, and she smiled and indicated that he should find a seat on a rock close by. There were rocks both large and small all along the shore of the lake, left by the glacier millions of years ago.

By the look on Reòll's face, she seemed to recognize him as a kindred spirit. They sat in silence for a long time, experiencing the beauty and serenity of the place when she began a conversation. He told her a little bit about his experience without revealing who he was and where he came from. She showed compassion for his loss of memory and began telling about herself.

"My name is Sarah Eliza Sigourney Cushing. My goodness, that is a mouthful, my friend, but that is who I am and proud of it." She smiled. "I have been coming here summers for a very long time. This is my favorite spot in the whole wide world. My husband was Edward Tuckerman. He was a professor of botany at Amherst College and an expert on lichens that are so prolific on this island. He died a few years ago, and I am very lonely." She lowered her head as she spoke of her husband. When she lifted her head again, she spoke softly. "I come here often to read poetry. That makes me feel at peace."

Reòll was empathetic and somewhat clairvoyant. He could feel her loneliness and wanted to help. He didn't know about poetry, but he wanted to learn, so he asked, "What is it you like to read? If it gives you pleasure, I would like to read it too, especially since I have no memories of my own."

She had a book beside her, and she lifted and read from it. Beautiful words brought him to tears.

> The bee is not afraid of me,
> I know the butterfly.
> The pretty people in the woods
> Receive me cordially.
> The brooks laugh louder when I come,
> The breezes madder play.
> Wherefore, mine eyes, thy silver mists?
> Wherefore, O summer's day?
> (Emily Dickinson)

She said, "This was written by a friend of mine. Her name was Emily Dickinson. My husband and I loved her very much."

As he listened to the words that she read, it was like she was reading his mind. That is the way he related to his new world. He felt at home with this beautiful person who was saying to him, "I am old and won't be able to come here much longer."

As she said those words, he had a vision of a beautiful stone bench in this very spot, in the future, that would memorialize her for all time. He told her what he saw.

She smiled and said, "Good! Then I can still come here and sit and enjoy this place with other people who will not even know I am here." She reached for his hand and said, "I hope we meet again."

He replied, "I'm sure we will."

He took his leave and began the walk up the slope toward the Pond House. As he walked toward the road, he began to have a sense of foreboding. "My goodness! Where is this unsettled feeling coming from?" He didn't like that sensation at all. With his back to the road, he looked toward the pond. The sky was bright with the afternoon sun, but in his mind's eye, clouds were gathering, and it became very dark. The pond looked almost black with crashing waves on the shore.

Suddenly, he began to shake, and he had a perception that something terrible was about to happen. He was aware of Cassie's visions and wondered if this lucid dream was related. In a moment, the premonition vanished, and he was delighted to see the sun on the mountains on the northern end of the pond and no sign of a disturbance on the water. The portent left him unsettled, however, and he was anxious to return home to his love. This time, he took the dirt road through the woods to the village. The way was faster than the path in the forest, though not quite so pretty. He began to run.

THE WEDDING

The day of the wedding finally arrived. Enough time on this earth plane passed for Reòll to have adjusted to being in a human body. He was still learning the oddities of human motives and emotions, but he accepted the strangeness of it all and looked forward to being with Cassie in a physical being. It was overwhelming. He trusted in the Almighty to make it all right.

The day was exquisite. A truly Maine day. A cool breeze blew in from the shore. The sky was the deepest blue one could imagine with fluffy white clouds. The temperature was just right, not too hot, and not too cold.

Most of the family came to the island in their buckboard with Chestnut leading the way. Aaron drove the vehicle carrying Mary and Foghorn, and they picked up Mae and Charles on the way. James sailed the peapod and brought Eddie Wind Eagle along with him. Everyone was almost giddy with excitement, although Mary was a bit nervous. She still was unsettled about the selkie situation and wondered what people would think.

Cassandra secured rooms for them at the boardinghouse. The inn, as a wedding gift, was giving them the very best rooms for a wedding present. She was usually a servant, but today and for a few days to come, she and Reòll would be honored guests.

Cassie cried when she saw the wedding dress. It was restored beautifully by Mary. Mrs. Anny Smith baked a beautiful cake with real flowers for a party after the wedding. Reverend McDonald gave them the usual talk about marriage and responsibility and how they should keep their faith and attend church regularly. They smiled as they left the preacher because they already knew all that and couldn't wait to be married.

It was late in the season. Most of the summer people had already left for the year, and that meant that everyone was free to enjoy the weather and some leisurely time. This wedding would be the last big bash of the season, and everyone was in a celebratory frame of mind.

Reòll and Cassie had a long walk on the beach in the morning. The guests had all arrived the day before and were sleeping late. Reòll and Cassie sat on the time rock, thinking of all that transpired in the last few months. It did not seem real. The marriage would take place about eleven in the late morning. A reception with lunch would follow at the inn. Then there would be a party with dancing.

They walked slowly back to the inn. Cassie kissed Reòll on the cheek and went to a dressing room with Mary to put on the dress that Mary had beautifully restored. First, there was the yards and yards of crinoline petticoats. Then the lace and lavender chemise that buttoned up the front. Over that were the organdy overskirts. There was a bustle pad that expanded and supported the fullness and drapery of her dress. Next, over the head came the dress, handsewn with tiny stitches. Made from sheer organdy from neck to shoulders and rimmed with a wide band and trimmed at the skirt, it formed a *V* in the front and back just below the bust. Ruffles topped the long off-the-shoulder sleeves that were narrow at the top and very full at the bottom. The dress had originally been an ivory color but was now a light amber because it was so old.

When it was time to go to the church, Mary brought forth a veil that she set on Cassie's head. The crown was ringed with pearls that were entwined with sea lavender and wild roses and draped all the way to the floor.

There was a knock on the door. Mary opened it, and there stood Nellie McIntire with an armload of flowers from the gardens. They were tied together with ribbons and lace and smelled divine. Cassie threw her arms around her and exclaimed at how beautiful the bouquet was and how sweet she was to bring it. She introduced her to Mary. Nellie smiled and kissed Cassie on the cheek and turned to Mary, saying, "I love your daughter. She brings joy wherever she goes, and we love her at the Pond House. We love Reòll too. He cares for the gardens and the flowers. These are beautiful because of him. I will leave you now. I see you are busy getting dressed. I will see you at the church. Bye-bye now."

"Bye, Nellie. Oh, by the way, is Marion here? Mama, Marion is Nellie's six-year-old daughter. Thank you again, Nellie."

"Yes! Marion is here. I left her on the beach. She is collecting wild rose petals for her flower-girl basket. She is so excited. She has never been in a wedding before. Good luck, my dear! You are a beautiful bride."

*****

Reòll was nearly beside himself with anticipation mixed with anxiety. He knew nothing about weddings, the culture, the traditions, the religious connotations. Most of all, he was nervous about being in front of all those people. He knew that they all loved them, but what would they think? Would he make mistakes? Would he drop the ring? Mary had given him the ring that was Catherine's wedding ring. It meant so much to her and to Cassie. The one thing he did understand was the love and commitment. He couldn't wait to see Cassie in that dress and for her to express her love to him for all eternity.

Aaron, James, and Eddie were with him, helping him get dressed and prepare. His new friends at the house where he stayed found him a proper tuxedo suit. He looked at himself in the floor-to-ceiling mirror and exclaimed, "I look like a penguin." He had seen them in the Boston aquarium. Somehow, he remembered them.

The men all laughed and patted him on the back. "We know it is difficult," acknowledged Aaron. "I know what you are going through. But as you can see, I lived through it, and you will too."

Soon the time came to leave for the church. It was only a short distance, but a carriage was brought around to the front of the inn. Cassie walked out into the sunshine, picked up her train, and with Mary's help, she carefully stepped up into the conveyance. The men walked to the church and were waiting inside. The church was full of guests, mostly people they worked with at the inn and Jordan Pond. But there were many locals there too. That was unusual because this was a summer church built for summer people. But today was special because so many people knew of Cassie and Reòll. They knew how they met, and it was so romantic. Of course, they did not even know the real story. But it was enough to know what they did know. They loved them and were enchanted. It was like a real-life fairy tale.

Music soon started playing.

Cassie stepped out of the carriage and heard someone whisper, "She's coming." As she stood in the entrance to the sanctuary, coming out of the bright sunshine, her eyes became accustomed to the dark room before her. The traditional wedding song was playing "The Bridal Chorus" from *Lohengrin* written by Wagner. Cassie loved that music. At home, she listened to it on her mother's wind-up Victrola. Mary had a collection of classical music and old recordings.

Cassie saw Reòll waiting for her in front of the Communion table with his best friend James, her brother, at his side. Aaron stepped beside her to escort her down the aisle. Tears began to flow down her cheeks. *That's okay,* she thought. *This is a very special day.*

Dancing down the aisle, spreading joy and rose petals in front of her along the red carpet, was little Marion McIntire. She had a lovely pink dress and a wreath of roses around her brow. She looked back at Cassie and smiled, then turned and danced on.

Soon Cassie was standing in front of Reverend McDonald. Reòll was holding both her hands in his, and they were repeating words spoken by the minister, and Reòll was slipping a ring upon her finger. Then the words were spoken. "You are now man and wife. You may kiss the bride."

She thought she would faint, but her father steadied her as Reòll embraced and kissed her. Then the music began again, and they ran up the aisle and out into the glorious, breathtaking island air, where they, in a daze, greeted everyone as they left the church.

Soon the carriage arrived to escort them back to the hotel where they would have lunch and a very nice party. They were both in a daze, wishing the day would go by faster. And it did!

UNION

Cassandra and Reòll gazed out of the upper-story window of the Seaside Inn, she with her back to him and her head resting on his shoulder, and he with his arm around her middle. They were both exhausted by the day's activities but feeling happier than either had felt in their entire lives. The inn left a bottle of champagne on the bedside table. Reòll popped the cork and filled two glasses that they held high so that the moonlight shone through the bubbles that mimicked the ocean water shimmering with the light. Reòll was reminded that the ocean was his realm. It was his world where he was most comfortable before he took on this most challenging persona of humanity. Here he stood with the ultimate goal of his mission, which he did not fully understand. And yet he felt that he was about to be fulfilled.

Cassandra was confused and shy, not knowing if she could live up to expectations. She knew that she and Reòll were destined to be together, but she did not know what that really meant, and she was scared.

As she sipped her champagne, she turned and looked up at Reòll. He could see her unease and embraced her, kissing her on the cheek. To lessen her anxiety, he said, "The first thing I need to do is get rid of this penguin suit, and I hope I never have to wear one again." He laughed nervously and a little too loudly.

Cassie smiled and stated matter-of-factly, "I will need help getting out of this dress. It may take all night just to unbutton all these tiny little fasteners."

Reòll gently replied, "That is something I can do to help." And he kissed her, not on the cheek this time but a breathtakingly long and tender kiss on the lips. She collapsed in his arms.

He continued unfastening the buttons and removing the layers and layers of crinoline, leaving the dress crumpled on the floor. After several minutes of anticipation, they stood holding hands, naked, fixing their eyes upon each other, like Adam and Eve without the serpent. They were so pure and innocent. They had that special eye contact many times, but never like this. It was like looking directly into the Source, into the soul, where the material world does not exist.

They both looked away, surprised, and then returned their gaze. They had never experienced anything like that in their lifetime, and Reòll had been here for a hundred years.

In a few seconds, all doubt and reluctance evaporated, and they came together. Time stood still. There was no time! They felt as though they were evaporating into pure energy. They were again eternal beings, dissolved into immortal consciousness. They became one soul in two bodies. They had always been so, but until this moment, they were unaware of the universal bond. Cassandra and Reòll were united at the Source and would be forever one. Life for them ascended. Their mission would be to spread love, joy, and hope to all and to help save and preserve this wonderful kingdom for which they were fortunate to be given. Such love does not come often in this existence, but when it does, it can light the world.

A New Life Begins

The newlyweds began their life together at the boardinghouse on Long Pond. They immediately started to look for a place of their own to live. There was a lovely piece of land about a mile down the road from the Pond House. A few other houses were there that had been moved from the Long Pond village. That would be a perfect location because it was close enough to walk to work if they could get a house built by next summer. The property was not considered valuable at this time, but as the rusticators bought up the land to build their cottages, it would not take long until it would be too expensive for them to purchase. So they had no time to lose. The place was not included in the reserve, so there was a good chance that they could secure it.

They walked toward the Jordan Pond House on the dirt road and stopped at one of the houses. Every one of the locals knew one another and were glad for the company, especially now that the season was ended.

They knocked on the door of the Allens, and Kathy Allen answered the door and invited them in. She told them that the land was owned by the Jordans, who previously owned the whole area around Jordan Pond and ran the sawmill before the McIntires took over, and they still cut ice on the pond in the winter.

Reòll said he would talk to them in the morning.

Kathy and her family knew of Cassie and Reòll, and she was delighted at the idea of having them as neighbors. The land was at the foot of Day Mountain, the local name for this medium-sized highland that had a number of trails and a beautiful view from the top. There was a frog pond on the land that would be full of peepers in the spring. A nice clearing was surrounded by a lovely forest. Across the dirt road, there was a newly planned-out cemetery, attractive and out of vision of anyone who didn't know it was there. It was carefully laid out, planted with shrubs and flowers, and well-cared for. It was said of this cemetery that the world has few spots of this kind so satisfying to all, and especially to those who have a personal interest in it.[16] It was created by George L. Stebbins,[17] a wealthy financier who was responsible for most of the recently developed new village of Seal Harbor. Cassandra knew him to be active, wise, and considerate with both summer visitors and local residents.

Mr. Dana, another wealthy summer person, expressed many times that there was nowhere on earth that can be found a home so beautiful and inspiring in scenery, hills, forests, cliffs, and lakes along with the boundless ocean views as Seal Harbor, Maine.

Cassie hadn't traveled the world much, but for what she knew of her home, she couldn't agree more. Reòll, coming from the sea, was still learning about the uniqueness and beauty. He was happy here.

It wasn't long before Cassandra found out she was going to have a baby. Now it was imperative that they find a place of their own. Life would be challenging, but they were so happy. Reòll definitely felt that part of his mission with Cassandra was to bring a new life into this realm. A life that would be half human and half omnipotent and eternal.

---

[16] As stated by Edward S. Dana in his notes about Seal Harbor.
[17] George Ledyard Stebbins was a wealthy real estate financier who developed Seal Harbor, Maine, and helped to establish Acadia National Park (Wikipedia).

Seal Harbor Supper

Reòll secured the land. He knew nothing about building but was grateful to be living in Seal Harbor where the men were happy to teach and spread their knowledge. Cassie always said that she recognized that this town was special. She appreciated the beauty and the environment, but growing up on the coast in a town that was also lovely, what she loved most about this place was the people. This community was exceptional in caring.

Cassie believed that the local folks in this village, though few in number, took care of one another. Once they got to know you, they watched over you and made sure you have what you need. Of course, it is expected that you pay it forward when the time comes. She was sure that even though they probably were unaware, it was one of the reasons the people from away wanted to live or vacation here. They knew that their help was necessary, and although patronizing, they wanted to make sure that once they secured what they needed, the land, the village, and the people were developed and safeguarded from exploitation and destruction and were protected for future generations. The strength and moral character of the locals, their honesty, and work ethic were unbreakable. No one went homeless or without being looked after. Reòll could attest to that.

Now he was beginning to learn what that means, going forward, for him and his family. He began clearing the land for a house and saw men from the town, who knew exactly what was needed, walking with their tools to instruct and help. They cut the trees and prepared the logs for the house and raised the timbers for the roof. The word spread, and others came. The women brought food and called for a community supper to raise funds for what they needed.

James and Eddie came from Down East to join in. Within a month, their log cabin was finished, and the community called for a housewarming.

Food and drinks were liberal—lobster stew, venison and deer meat, bean salad and baked beans, brown bread, and the ubiquitous gelatin salad. They cleared a place in the living area of the house so that they could dance. Improvised musical instruments magically appeared, and almost every family had a daughter who could sing. This time of year, especially on a Saturday night, it was time to have a party or a dance.

A garden was planted out front of the house, and food for the coming winter was abundant. Cassie planted flowers and fruit trees for the future. Deer were plentiful. Reòll and Cassandra were grateful beyond words and spent the fall and winter awaiting their newborn. It was a peaceful time for them that they spent with new friends and neighbors, a time for Thanksgiving and Christmas and to build new traditions for their family in this perfectly wonderful place.

*****

The baby was due in June. That meant that Cassie would not be able to work at the inn next summer. Reòll would ask Mr. McIntire for a hosting job as well as taking care of the gardens so that Cassie could stay home with the baby. Of course, Mary would come and help when the time came.

SAVE OUR SEALS

Reòll had a new concern. He was worried about the seals in the harbor. He still felt like he needed to take care of them. He loved them and felt like he was still one of them. They were diminishing in large numbers due to the fishermen shooting them to keep them from stealing their catch. Some people killed them for their pelts. There were very few gray and harbor seals left in the harbor since his transformation. During the cold weather, he remembered going south, but each summer, upon return, there were fewer in the harbor. His pod was quickly becoming extinct. This broke his heart. He was aware of their diminishing numbers when he lived among them, and now that he was human, he hoped he would be able to help restore them to a healthy population. He understood the Native Americans taking them for food and even their personal clothing. That he could understand. But just random killing or taking them for their pelts to sell for profit was not acceptable. For a while there was even a bounty paid for killing them. He had to do something if he could.

He emphasized to those who would listen that the seals needed to be protected from entanglement and that they needed a place to live that has minimal human impact and an elevation needed to survive. The haul-out ledges just beyond Seal Harbor offered both, with little to no people contact and a proper environment needed for survival. He hoped and prayed for laws to be enacted in the future that ensured that the public cannot disturb marine mammals.

"Seals are lovable and intelligent. They are fascinating." He persuaded those he was attempting to convince by being himself lovable while saying, "Who doesn't love seals? Let us live up to our name Seal Harbor, Maine."[18]

---

[18] The Marine Mammal Protection Law was not enacted until 1972, long after marine mammals were hunted and killed for years, essentially erasing them from the New England waters. Now penalties for violation of the act can be up to one-year imprisonment; civil penalties up to $11,000; and forfeiture of a vessel involved, including penalties for that vessel up to $25,000; according to NOAA. In 2017, a Maine boat captain was sentenced to three days in jail

He spent a lot of time at the wharf talking to the lobstermen and fishermen when they docked their boats. He also talked to the wealthy folks, especially summer folks, who stayed the winter or who came for short visits off season. He discussed a lot about the seals and how the summer people liked seeing them.

"Why would one name a harbor Seal Harbor, and then not have any seals to observe and love? That just doesn't make sense." He attempted to convince people who had influence in getting and making legislation to work toward restoring the seals in the harbor.

He also applauded and encouraged the children of the town who, during the summer months, set up a lemonade stand on the beach with a sign that said "SAVE OUR SEALS." They were so passionate because they found a seal pup washed up on the beach that had been shot. The local newspapers published pictures of them, and they raised quite a bit of money that they contributed to others who were working for conservation, and they raised awareness of the near extinction of the beloved mammals.

Reòll was so proud of them. He knew it would take time for things to improve, and he knew that he would probably not be around long enough to see the change. He also firmly believed that this advocacy was part of his mission, and he was compelled to save his seal beings. He was sure he could make a difference for the long run. He had to try.

When he wasn't saving the seals, in the winter months, he spent time adapting to the ice and snow. It was so much different than his life in the sea when he went south to the aquarium in Boston for the extreme cold weather. When it wasn't snowing, he spent time out of doors clearing his land and enjoying his family. He missed his fur hide but was grateful for the knitted hats and scarves and mittens

---

and ordered to pay a $1,000 fine for shooting and killing a seal off the coast of Acadia National Park, as reported by the *Portland Press Herald* (https://bangordailynews.com/2018/07/02).

"Seals Were Once Nearly Wiped Out from the Gulf of Main: Here's How They Were Brought Back," *Seacoast Online*, July 2, 2018.

This outcome would have made Reòll really happy, but I bet he knows.

provided by the Ladies' Aid Society, actually named the Golden Rule Society, which was a part of the local church in this community.

The days passed quickly, and he looked forward to spring and helping get the Pond House ready for the summer season. And of course, he was excited and very anxious about the new baby that would be here soon. The whole village was anticipating the arrival. Would it be a boy or a girl? What would their name be? It was almost time. He and Cassie spent many hours thinking about a name.

Cassie suggested, "If it is a boy, we can name him Gabriel, and if a girl, she could be Gabriella. Gabriel was my great-grandfather's name. He was Catherine's father, who brought our family to America. He is very important in our family history, and it will be an honor for him and for our baby to be named after him. Gabriel is a biblical name mentioned many times in the Bible. It means 'devoted to God,' 'God is my strength.' What could be more appropriate than that?"

Reòll nodded and smiled. "That is a perfect name for our child. I love it. So it is settled."

Reòll Laughs

Reòll seemed to adapt to humanity pretty well, at least on the outside, although he was daily beset by emotions and unexpected societal norms that kept him constantly alert and off guard. One of the things that he discovered he needed upon his arrival was the ability to read. There were so many subtleties needed for smooth and amiable communication with others. He had so much to learn. Fortunately, he still had the ability to communicate telepathically with those who were recipients, and that translated very well in understanding the written word.

Cassie recognized the need and began immediately teaching him to read. He had a photographic mind and memory so that he learned very quickly.

One of his favorite places to hang out was the Seal Harbor Library. It was only a few years old. It was built and dedicated to the village by George Ledyard Stebbins, who was a cofounder and library president. Mr. Stebbins was a quiet, gentle man who dedicated his life to the good of the village. He was a renowned scientist and very wealthy real estate financier who developed Seal Harbor and was responsible for a smooth transition from the village of Long Pond to Seal Harbor. Reòll always nodded and greeted him with a smile when they met on the street, and Mr. Stebbins always tipped his hat and returned the smile.

Reòll had a great respect for these wealthy residents who not only met their own needs but also developed and put in place sustainable plans to assure that the town would grow in a way to benefit all, both at present and in the future. Now here was this wonderful library, a source of endless knowledge that was kept stocked with the classics and the most up-to-date literature available.

Reòll spent at least an hour a day at the library reading and discussing his newfound knowledge with others. He found this was a wonderful way to become acquainted with the villagers and wealthy residents alike.

Today was the beginning of April. In Maine, on such a day, one didn't know whether to dress in short sleeves, ditch the winter coat, or don the muck boots and expect snow. The weather was unpredictable. This day, the sun was shining brightly, and it was quite warm.

Reòll was sitting in the library enjoying the latest acquisition when a fisherman burst through the door, beckoning the occupants to come outside. As Reòll stepped out into the sunlight, the fisherman shouted, "Come to the dock and see the fifty-pound lobster that was caught this morning!"

Reòll was very excited to see this phenomenon from his world, and he dashed toward the dock that was across the road to the left and only a short way from the library. When he arrived, there was a number of lobstermen standing around with their heads bowed and one hand covering their mouth. They were glancing toward the town to see who was coming to see their catch, and they seemed to be chuckling.

Reòll arrived and called out, "Where is the fifty-pound lobster that was just caught?"

Everyone started laughing and slapping their sides.

Reòll insisted, "Let me see the catch."

All the onlookers laughed even harder, enjoying making fun of Reòll, who was so innocent. They all shouted in unison, "April Fools'! April Fools'!"

Reòll could see they were all enjoying a prank at his expense, and he didn't understand. He felt bewildered, humiliated, offended, and all kinds of negative emotions that were new and uncomfortable. He turned and ran up the road and back to the library where it was quiet and peaceful. He did not know about humor. It was foreign to him. He did not know about making fun of someone or practical jokes. He was too kind to do that.

When he regained his composure, he went outside and walked quickly up the main street and, at the top of the hill, turned left onto the Jordan Pond Road toward home where he knew Cassie would be waiting, and she would be there to comfort and explain.

She was watching for him as he approached on the path leading to the house. She could see he was upset and distressed, and she went outside and walked slowly toward him. She didn't hurry because she was heavy with child.

"Whatever is wrong, my darling?" she exclaimed as she threw her arms around him.

Seeing her always raised his spirits, and he kissed her forehead and patted her baby belly. He couldn't help but smile. "Let's go inside, and I will tell you what happened this morning. I am in a quandary, and I hope you can shed some light on the events and explain some things to me."

They entered the house that smelled of pine wood and smoke from the fireplace that was built from sea stones, rounded from eons of surf washing them against one another.

"First, tell me how you are feeling today? Is the baby kicking and jumping?" That brought a smile, and his solemn expression vanished.

"I am feeling wonderful. Our little one lets me know frequently that he or she is strong and healthy and almost ready to emerge. I am a little scared but getting ready for the little rascal to arrive."

Hand in hand, they walked to the long seat where they could sit together. They sat down, and Reòll began relating what occurred. He showed all kinds of emotions while telling his story and ended by saying, "This makes me so angry and humiliated, and I don't understand why. Can you explain to me why everyone laughed at me, and what do they mean by April Fools'? I am not a fool, and I never got to see the giant lobster."

Cassie replied, "You are not a fool. Those people at the dock did not intend to hurt your feelings. They were playing a joke that was meant to be funny, and it was not meant just for you. It was a group practical joke meant for the town on this special day that happens each year called April Fools' Day. This tells me that there is one very important expression that you need to learn, and believe me, you will like it. You need to learn to laugh!"

"What is a laugh?"

"Well, let me just say that humor and laughter have very positive effects on our health and happiness. Do you remember telling me about the author that you read last week at the library? The book was written by a philosopher named Nietzsche. He said, 'Not through wrath but through laughter one slayeth.' In other words, if one can find the humor, what's funny, in a situation and make people laugh instead of lashing out in anger, one can turn an uncomfortable situation into something that relieves the tension and settles the competition. When we expect a certain outcome and something unexpected happens, it relieves the unease and makes us laugh. The fishermen were playing a joke. They were all in on it and expected you to fall for it. You wanted to see the lobster that did not exist. You fell for the joke, and that made everyone in on the joke laugh. They had no idea that you didn't know about April Fools' Day.

"Humor is inclusive and expresses a human need. One might say, it is the oil that gets us through the day. Everyone can get in on a joke. That's kind of what happened on the dock. The problem was that you were not in on it and didn't even know about April 1 as Fools' Day. Therefore, everyone in on it felt closer, but you became a victim because you were not in on the joke. It made you sad instead of becoming self-aware. You were being tricked and fell for it and could not laugh with the group, making you feel humiliated and angry.

"Did you know that babies laugh before they can speak? People of all cultures laugh. Even apes laugh. Laughter is a universal human language. It is a shared expression of relief at the passing of danger. It can be a reaction to a sense of loneliness and mortality that only humans feel, and that would explain why this is so new and unknown to you. I hope my soliloquy makes you feel better and gives you something new and important to experience. Now I am going to give you a test.

"How do you get a squirrel to like you?"

"I don't know. How?"

"Act like a nut."

Reòll looked bewildered for a moment. He thought about what Cassie unexpectedly said, and when he got the punch line, he laughed out loud.

Then she said, "How do we know that the ocean is friendly?"

He shook his head, and she replied, "It waves."

This time he laughed from his toes and said, "Enough! I get it." And he became self-aware, sad, but satisfied, seeing the humor in his not getting the joke about the fish.

He giggled some more and stated, "I would have liked to see the fifty-pound lobster though." He laughed and laughed. "I think I better spend more time at the library and study some more philosophers."

With that, he embraced Cassie, and they laughed together, and he felt so much better.

MAY DAY

Summer was fast approaching, and Reòll was becoming excited about spring and the coming baby. Every human experience was new to him and at times overwhelming. He had so much to learn.

One of his favorite pastimes was to hang out with the local kids in the village. He spent a lot of time at the schoolhouse in Bracy Cove, Little Long Pond. It was called Knowledge Hill and was sometimes used as a winter church and meeting place. Reòll and Cassie spent a lot of time there during the winter months, which were long and lonely.

The town kids were so much fun and knew so much about being human. Now it was almost May, and after his time at the library, he walked along the beach on the dirt road to the school. Snow was falling lightly, and he thought, *Why isn't it warming up?* He longed for sun and new leaves on the trees and flowers.

As he entered the school, he saw the children with a teacher who was instructing them how to make what looked like colorful containers. He asked if he could watch.

"Of course, you can."

They all loved Reòll. He had more in common with the children than most grown-ups. He was always full of questions that they could answer, and it made them feel really important.

"Come, sit with us, and we will teach you how to make May baskets and tell you all about the tradition. May Day is one of our favorite times of celebration."

He found a place out of the way and sat down cross-legged on the floor where he could watch. "What are May baskets?" he asked.

The teacher, Mrs. Walls, replied, "We make these by hand each year. We fold paper into cones. Then we paste narrow strips of paper together to make handles. We find pretty colored paper or cloth, sometimes lace if we can find some, to cover the cones. Here"—she handed him paper and scraps of cloth—"we will show you how it is done."

This is really fun, he thought as he reached out to gather the paper and trimmings. "Then what do you do with these lovely containers when they are made?"

"We fill them with candy and treats and flowers if we can find them."

"What do you do after that? It looks like there will be a lot of them when you are finished."

Mrs. Walls smiled. "Let me tell you about this tradition. The custom is usually for a child and sometimes for a romantic who is in love. They hang the basket on the doorknob and shout, 'May basket!' Then they run and hide and watch for their friend or lover to come to the door. If the person who brought the basket to the door gets caught, they are entitled to a kiss."

Reòll exclaimed, "I would love to play this trick on Cassie. She is so tired of winter and is awaiting our baby. She needs some cheering up. Please tell me where this custom came from." He loved to hear tales of why people celebrated the way they do.

Mrs. Walls replied, "This lovely tradition had its origins in Roman times. Do you know about Romans?"

"Yes! I do. I have been reading about world history in the library. I am learning so much."

She began by saying, "The Romans had a spring festival of the goddess of flowers whose name was Flora. And in Germany, it was in remembrance of Saint Walburga, who helped Saint Boniface bring Christianity to that country in the eighth century. Ladies would secretly place roses or rice in the shape of a heart at the doorstep of their beloved."

"So when did this practice come to Maine?" he asked.

"Well," she explained, "it has been very popular in New England, and that includes Maine, in the last century and this new century. There is an author named Louisa May Alcott who wrote about them in her 1880s children's book called *Jack and Jill.* That is a book you might like to read. She has written other books. I think you would enjoy them. I have a copy here that I will read to you. It is lovely to contemplate.

"'Such a twanging of bells and rapping of knockers; such a scampering of feet in the dark,' she wrote. She described 'droll collisions as boys came racing round corners, or girls ran into one another's arms as they crept up and down steps on the sly.'

"'Such laughing, whistling, flying about of flowers and friendly feeling—it was almost a pity that Mayday did not come oftener.'"

Mrs. Walls stated passionately, "You must make something with your hands from a thing that takes shape in your heart. Something with color and sugar, and if you're doing it right, a little fear. And then—and this should be the hardest part—you have to let go and take your first step across the lawn, toward the closed door that suddenly seems far away. Then you knock and then you run but not too fast. I hope this is all making sense to you."

"Oh yes! It sounds like an adventure and fun."

After a while, his beautiful basket was finished. Mrs. Walls gave him treats and handmade paper flowers for him to fill it with. She said, "You can leave it here until the first of May that we call May Day. We will keep it for you in the closet, and you can retrieve it before you go home after your library visit."

He was so happy to have made a treasure with his own hands. That was something new to him, and he loved spending the afternoon with the children. He thanked Mrs. Walls and the kids and stepped outside into the chill and snow.

Several days later, it was May first. The day was cold and dreary. He spent the morning at the library reading Louisa May Alcott. He cried when Beth died in *Little Women* and realized again how sad and heavy mortality can be.

Drying his eyes, he left the library, and his spirits rose again as he dashed off to the schoolhouse to collect his May basket. On his way home, he was careful to hide his gift. The weather was not that good, and he didn't want it to be spoiled before he reached his house.

As he approached home, which was nestled in among the trees, he was careful that no one would see him. He looked from side to side and then tiptoed up to the front door, hung the basket by the handle, and shouted, "May basket!" as loud as he could, knocking on the door. Then he ran and hid behind the nearest tree.

Cassie opened the door, and her mouth dropped open as she saw the basket and treats. She knew about May Day and was laughing as she looked around and spotted him hiding. She rushed as fast as she could to catch him, knowing that he would not run away. And she grabbed him and hugged him, and that wasn't an easy thing to do with her large baby belly. They kissed passionately, and he was as happy as he had ever been. Today was a good day to be human. He laughed. This would be a day to remember.

Spring Comes Slowly

After the first of May, Reòll began watching for signs of spring. Every day that went by was closer to the birth of their baby. He had a dilemma though. He wanted to stay home and spend as much time with Cassandra as he could, but it was also time to go to work at the Pond House to get ready to welcome the college students who would be arriving soon and would stay for the summer to work. There was so much to do to prepare for the season that would begin on Declaration Day, the thirtieth of May.

Presently, it was approaching the second week of May. The sky was bluer every day that wasn't raining or sometimes even snowing. Almost overnight, the landscape turned white and pink with blossoms from the shadbush trees, a member of the rose family.

Reòll, always curious, asked Cassie, "How did the trees get such an interesting name?"

"Grandmother remembered them from when she lived farther south in New England and was delighted that they also grew here in Maine. The trees were so welcome each year because they were the first to bloom each spring. Farther south, they blossomed at the same time that the shad fish returned to spawn. And that is how they got their name."

"Tell me about shad fish."

"The shad are a schooling fish, and thousands are often seen on the surface of rivers and streams in the spring. They are a member of the herring family. You must remember herring from your ocean world." She smiled, remembering his otherworldly experiences. "They also are known by another more somber name of serviceberry, named such because they bloom directly after the winter thaw, signifying that the time has come for burial services after the deep freeze of winter."

She continued, enjoying the memories of her beloved grandmother.

"These trees bloom before there is any foliage in the forest. They have a lovely fragrance and are early pollinators for native and honeybees. The Native Americans dried the berries and mixed them with venison and bear fat to make pemmican."[19]

Reòll mused, "Eddie Wind Eagle brought me some pemmican the last time he visited. It was interesting, to say the least. I am beginning to develop a taste for it, and it comes in really handy when I need to be out in the woods or walking to town when it is winter. I like it."

That led to another subject. Cassie was loath to bring it up, but it was important to prepare. She said to Reòll, "When the shadbush blooms, it is a harbinger of a terrible little critter that we call the blackfly. Some people think it is the same as the shad fly, for which the tree is named. But that is not true. They emerge at the same time. The shad fly swarms, is a nuisance, but it does not bite. The blackfly, however, loves to feed on people. There are several species, some of which prefer other mammals and birds. It is the females that bite. They need running water to survive, so you need to be careful where it is wet. They do help keep our waterways clean, but that is small consolation. Please be cautious because you cannot always feel them when they bite. Eddie told me that rubbing bear grease on your skin helps keep them away, but since we don't have ready access to bear or bear fat, I would recommend you cover your arms and head when the shadbush blooms. The blackflies are only around for a few weeks' time. By the Fourth of July, they are gone. Thus ends the lesson for the day."

---

[19] Pemmican was a concentrated mixture of lean venison meat and bone marrow dried over a slow fire until it was hard and brittle. It was pounded with stones until it reached a powdered consistency and then mixed with melted fat. Dried berries were added and also pounded into powder and mixed with the meat, making a nutritious meal.

DECORATION DAY

Cassie was right. The blackflies were gruesome. However, Reòll was enjoying the outcome of spring. After the shad bloomed, then came the cherry blossoms. Then everything seemed to burst into bloom at once. The wild rhodora was everywhere in the woods where it was damp and along the dirt roads as long as there was plenty of sunshine.

The Indian moccasin flowers were everywhere in the woods surrounding their house. When Eddie was visiting, he told him how his people called them by that name. Like his tribe, they were opposed to any attempts at civilization. As people from Europe became more ubiquitous in America and Mount Desert Island, the moccasin flowers transformed into lady slippers. The flowers were delicate and did not transplant well. They were to be seen and not disturbed.

In the forest next to their house, there were also many small fragrant white flowers that were blooming everywhere. Cassie picked some and brought them into the house because they smelled so good.

"What are these called?" asked Reòll.

"I think the official name is trailing arbutus, but we just call them May flowers because they are often the first flowers to bloom in the spring. After a long winter, they are God's blessing."

Then it was the thirtieth of May, Declaration Day, which commemorated the soldiers who died during the Civil War, the War Between the States. It was a sad time of remembrance for Cassie, who lost her grandfather and two great-uncles during the conflict.

Reòll wondered why that day each year was chosen. Cassie explained that the day was picked because it was not the anniversary of any particular battle as there were many. They also chose a time when flowers would be in bloom in the north. It seemed an appropriate time.

May 30 was the official beginning day of summer on Mount Desert Island. The hotels were full of the first summer guests, and Seal Harbor was preparing for the Declaration Day commemoration ceremony that was to be held at the town dock at noon.

Mary and Aaron with James and Foghorn arrived in the morning with the buckboard and Chestnut. They brought the larger vehicle because they all wanted to attend the ceremony together.

Cassie was over the moon with excitement to see her family, and they were happy to see that she lived in such a lovely place. Her garden out front was newly planted, and Reòll with Eddie's help had planted apple trees on both sides of the house.

Cassie freshly baked bread and lobster stew and popovers for lunch, in honor of the Jordan Pond House opening, with strawberry jam and freshly churned butter for dessert. They ate the meal early so that they would be on time for the meeting at the dock.

When they were finished with lunch, they all climbed into the buckboard and slowly made their way through the forest, on the Jordan Pond Road, past the Seal Harbor Cemetery, and were soon passing between the newly-built homes or those that were moved from Little Long Pond. Soon they were on Main Street, passing the Glen Cove House and continuing toward the ocean and the intersection of Main Street and the drive that ended at the steamboat wharf. They found a place to park their conveyance and tied Chestnut to a bar meant for horses and walked slowly to the end of the dock.

Cassie was tired and found a bench to sit upon while they waited for the ceremony to start. Quite a few summer people and some locals arrived, some wearing military uniforms and some carrying large flags. Women had flowers.

Cassie made a wreath out of pine boughs interwoven with May flowers and blossoms and tied together with a black ribbon. It was lovely.

At noon, the ritual began. A young boy from the village stepped forward with a horn and began playing "Taps." Then several people stepped forth to speak of the war. Some had family members who served, and they spoke solemnly of the sacrifices made.

Near the end of the service, Cassie stepped forward toward the end of the pier and asked if she could speak. The master of ceremonies nodded and beckoned her forward. She turned and faced the crowd.

In a clear voice, she stated that her grandfather, Samuel O'Conner, his brother Daniel O'Conner, and her uncle James Clark died in the war. Samuel died a hero at the Battle of Antietam. Uncle James fell at Cemetery Ridge at Gettysburg, and her uncle Daniel O'Conner died in a hospital in Virginia from his wounds.

"I have a letter that I would like to read, if I may."

"Thank you, young lady. We will be honored to hear your presentation."

She began reading slowly and then with passion and determination.

"This letter to my grandmother from Daniel was written on this day of December 15, 1862:

Dear Catherine,

It is with heavy heart that I write to tell you of Samuel's death. By the time you receive this letter, I'm certain that you will have received a telegram with the sad news. I will describe to you what happened because I want you and Mary to know that Samuel died a hero. On December 13, we watched line after line of brave men march up the hill toward the rebels and suffer heavy casualties.

Then we advanced under heavy fire of grapeshot, canister, and bullets. Our advance was slowed by the bodies of our comrades piled upon one another. We took a position along a picket fence several yards from the Confederate positions.

We forged ahead again and again, beaten back by close-range rifle fire. The Irish brigade pushed on beyond all former charges. We took cover in a small depression with a two-foot-high fence where we could blaze away at the rebels and where we stayed and continued the barrage. At one point, our beloved flag fell to the ground. Samuel, who was slightly wounded, left the cover of the fence and rushed to pick up the flag, running in the forefront, encouraging some of the men to follow. Some of them sidled over to an abandoned brick house, continuing the fire until their ammunition was gone, while Samuel and other Irishmen continued the run up the bloody slope following the colors. At dusk, I, along with other survivors, still by the fence, fell back to the town of Fredericksburg. At that point, I did not know where Samuel was. Colonel Byrnes stood by the colors, trying to determine if there was anything left of his regiment. The Irish brigades lost two-thirds of its numbers, 158 of the Twenty-Eighth. General Sumner, commander of the II Corps, rebuked a man for not being with his company, to which he replied, "This *is* all my company, sir."

We remained that night and the next day at the base of the hill. It was bitter cold, and we were unable to reach our fallen men due to the hostile fire. We remained in Fredericksburg for two days, expecting a counterattack that never came. During that last day, I ventured out to look for Samuel. I found him still clutching the tattered green flag. I picked him up and cradled him in my arms, overcome with grief. I found the letter he wrote on December 13 in his pocket. I knew you would want it even though it was bloodied by the bullet that pierced his heart. At least I do not believe that he suffered but died instantly. Sad to say this horrible battle was a fruitless effort. We have paid a gruesome price and still no victory. I am more determined than ever to make the damn rebels pay for what they have done.

I am so sorry, Catherine.

Love always,
Daniel

Cassie stepped over to the bench, picked up her wreath, and walked to the edge of the dock. She turned and asked those gathered to repeat the Lord's Prayer, and as they were reciting it, she turned and tossed the wreath into the water and watched it slowly drift out to sea with the tide.

She turned and said, "Thank you for listening," and slowly walked back to the bench and sat down.

Mary, with tears in her eyes, put her arms around her daughter and planted a kiss on her forehead, so proud of her.

There were many tears and sad expressions. Then the master of the service asked Reverend McDonald to end with a prayer.

The family then walked to the edge of the pier and watched as the wreath disappeared behind a boat. It was time to go home. And they did.

HERE COMES GABRIEL

It was the second week in June. The rusticators were filling the beaches and trails and tea lawn at Jordan Pond despite the blackflies. Reòll reluctantly went to work every day, reporting in at eleven just in time to greet lunch guests.

Aaron and James went back to the farm, leaving Mary and Foghorn to stay with Cassie, who was close to term, uncomfortable and excited to meet Gabriel or Gabriella. The family arranged for a local midwife, Louine Walton, to come and assist with the birth. Since there was no way to get in touch, she decided to spend a few weeks with the family for the wait, and hopefully, it would not be much longer.

Cassie was happy to have Foghorn with her. She and Mary borrowed a neighbor's horse and buggy every day to ride to the Pond House and show Foghorn where Reòll spent his days so that when the time came for the baby to arrive, he could fetch him to come home.

That day soon arrived. It was a beautiful, warm day, and Cassie knew that the baby was coming. Louine suggested that it would be quite a long while before the baby was born, but Mary thought it wise to send Foghorn for Reòll right away because babies in their family had a way of arriving quickly. She hoped that would be the case for Cassandra.

Cassie opened the door and whispered in Foghorn's ear, "Go get Reòll and bring him home."

With that, Foghorn took off on a run, making dust as he ran up the Jordan Pond Road toward Jordan Pond.

He arrived in a short time and ran up to the front door barking. Reòll was inside greeting guests and heard the woofing. He recognized that it was Foghorn, and he asked Mr. McIntire if he could leave. Everyone became excited knowing that the baby was coming.

Thomas patted him on the back and said, "Go quickly, and good luck."

Reòll grabbed his jacket from the coat tree and burst out the door, and he and Foghorn took off on a run.

"Come on, boy. We need to go."

It didn't take long for them to round the bend and onto the path to their front door. They could hear Cassie crying out, and that scared them.

The women met them at the door and ushered Reòll into the bedroom, where it was apparent that things were progressing as they should—and quickly. Reòll took Cassie's hand and kissed it. He leaned over just as she cried out again, and tears began to flow down his cheeks because she was in such pain.

In a minute, Cassie smiled and said, "I'm okay. This is what is supposed to happen. Now don't you worry. I will be all right."

Louine said, "You can stay here if you can be supportive and not be disruptive. She is doing fine, and the baby will be here soon."

He agreed, wiped the tears, kissed Cassie on the forehead, and sat quietly, holding her hand that she squeezed until it hurt.

About an hour later, Cassie gave one loud cry, and Mary said, "*Push!*" Cassie did, and the baby was out, screaming and kicking wildly. Louine took a warm cloth and washed him. The baby was a him! Then she wrapped him in a blanket and put him in his father's arms.

Reòll wept again. He cradled Gabriel, who stopped crying, and one could imagine he gazed up at him as if to say, "I'm here, Dad."

The women looked at one another and whispered, "Did you see his feet?"

Mary nodded, and Louine said, "He has webbed toes. I have never seen that before."

Mary replied, "Yes, I can see that. I would ask you not to tell anyone because we don't want him to have a stigma or for anyone to make fun of him."

Louine replied, "My lips are sealed. He is a beautiful baby."

Reòll examined Gabriel's toes and knew exactly where they came from. Gabriel was his father's son after all.

Cassie was exhausted but happy beyond words. Reòll put the baby in her arms, and they both hugged him and wept.

Gabriel was born, half human and half eternal, omnipotent, and full of love. He was a very special boy.

The Years Passed Quickly

Cassie was a good mom and spent as much time as she could with Gabriel. She took up her previous working relationship with the Seaside Inn when he was old enough to accompany her with her duties as a maid. One of the things she loved about working in Seal Harbor was that the wealthy people never referred to their help as servants. They were always called the help, those people who helped them through their summers on the island. Cassie and the other helpers never felt belittled or lost their dignity. And indeed, the locals were proud and dignified.

She also took on duties like cleaning the summer church and helping with the church school. She was sad that the children from the hill did not mingle with the local kids. However, she tried to include all the children in the village, rich or poor, in the youth group and Sunday school. She felt it was her mission to bring folks together, and integrating the young people was a good place to start.

On Sunday morning, she gathered together the kids and took them to the beach where they could sit on the rocks and have a short Bible study and then collect sand dollars and sea urchins. Sometimes they took their findings to the other winter church at Long Pond and made art out of their treasures. They sold them to earn money for a fund that helped with buying craft supplies, or they saved it to help people in the village when they got sick or had special needs. Often, they gave their earnings to the church for missions.

Spending time with the McIntires and their special love for the outdoors was a favorite pastime, and Cassie felt like the time spent protecting the island from exploitation was part of her mission. Reòll felt the same.

THE SPLIT ASH BASKET

> Glooskap, a great and powerful being, came to the Dawn Land, the land of the sunrise, the home of the Wabanaki. There were no Indians here then…only wild bands far off, Elves and little men, rock dwellers. Out of these, he made Humans. He shot at the Ash trees, the basket trees, with his bow and arrows, and out of the bark came the Indians.[20]

Eddie Wind Eagle came to visit often. He loved spending time with Reòll. He knew that they were kindred spirits, maybe even soulmates. Reòll loved hearing about Eddie's tribe and the myths and legends that he was so willing to share, especially those myths that guided Cassie through the time that she had a mystery to solve because of a recurring vision. If it weren't for Eddie and his grandmother, she and Foghorn might not have saved Mary and Mae from that impending disaster.

Eddie always said, "It is difficult to gain understanding from those who have not experienced second sight. In your society, you do not have many people who are respected for their gift of prophecy. It is different in my culture. My grandmother is the medicine woman of my clan. She is very wise. She is a descendant of Mary Nicola,[21] whom everyone called Molly Molasses because she was so sweet. By her own telling, she was born in a canoe and grew up talking to the little people known to us as Mikum-wasus (pronounced "Meek-gum-waz-zus"). Molly went to these all-powerful magic medicine people or Medowlinu (pronounced "Meh-dow-len-oo"), who taught her about medicine and helped her when she needed their power and

---

[20] Inspired by Katy Kelleher (, September 2020).

[21] Bunny McBride and Harald E. L. Prins, *Indians in Eden: Wabanakis and Rusticators on Maine's Mt. Desert Island* (Camden, Maine: Down East Books, 2009), 45; Acacia Artisans, Stories and Facts, http://www.acaciart.com/stories/archive13.html.

strength. They also taught her sacred and ancient songs and dances to control the elements and the environment and how to cure ailments. She was a great healer and helped many people. It is said she could hex a person by a mere glance if they were unkind. She had the power to look inside a person to see their ailment, remove it, and take it into her own body. She also knew songs to rid herself of her own ailments so that she would not become ill. She died in 1867, the year my grandmother was born. For all these reasons, I believe in my grandmother's wisdom."

Reòll was sure Eddie could help with Cassie's recent visions that she was plagued by. He knew because of his own ability to see into the future that he would somehow be involved in saving her from disaster. He hoped that Eddie would be able to help.

It was Reòll's day off from work, and he was at home working in the garden and doing repairs around the house when he saw Eddie Wind Eagle coming up the path toward him. Eddie was such a handsome young man. He was of medium stature, had long black braids, and was wearing a wide-brimmed hat with a feather tucked into a leather band. He was carrying a beautiful split ash basket.

Eddie handed the pack basket to Reòll, who asked, "Eddie, how was this made?"

Eddie, always pleased to tell stories, began to relate a legend given to a great leader of his ancestors who was concerned for the future of their people. He shared, "The black ash basket came in a vision of Black Elk, who was nearing the end of his time on earth and wanted to leave his people with something to teach them both patience and a means to provide for their families. He asked the Creator what he could do, and the Creator answered that when he died, they should bury his ashes where they would grow a special tree. He was to instruct his people to protect and look after this tree that was sacred and keep it from harm. When the tree matured, the people were instructed to cut it down and pound the tree, removing the growth rings that separated into strips. Then he showed them how to weave the strips into baskets. Before Black Elk died, he taught the people how to weave the baskets. He now knew that this would teach them patience and a means to provide for their families by sell-ing the baskets. He was grateful to the Creator for the vision and for teaching his community how to survive."

Reòll said, "I have seen these baskets on sale at the Pond House and have wanted one. This will be so helpful when I am walking to work or to the village."

Eddie replied, "I know! I have been concerned. I am aware that you are worried about Cassie and her visions. I know that you will be needing this basket soon."

"Whatever do you mean?"

"You will know soon enough. Now let me help you pick those beans. Do you think I could stay for supper?"

Reòll grinned. "You know better than to ask. Of course, Cassie and Gabriel will be home soon, and she will be so happy to see you."

CASSIE'S DREAMS

Cassie was so happy with Reòll and Gabriel, happier than she ever imagined. She loved their log cabin, the garden, her job, the village children, working with the McIntires, and Reòll was the love of her life. For most of the first few years that they were together, she did not have nightmares. But recently, they returned. She would wake up screaming and be embarrassed. No amount of comfort would make her feel better.

Reòll was worried. He would cradle her in his arms and ask, "What did you see, my dear?"

She would reply, "I was near a body of water. There was a rainbow in the sky, and suddenly, it grew dark...very dark. Thunder and lightning began crashing, and the wind began to blow so hard that the rain went sideways, and I couldn't see. Suddenly, I was in the water with a child, and I was spinning. The boy was clutching at me, and we were going down, down, down. Then there was a creature circling around us, and I lost consciousness. That's all I remember. It is always the same, and it is terrifying. I can't breathe. I think I might drown."

Reòll stated matter-of-factly, "I have talked with Eddie about these dreams, and he says don't worry! Everything will be all right."

Cassie asked, "How can he possibly know that?"

Reòll said, "It's because he knows stuff. If he says it will be okay, then it will. You are not to worry."

"Okay, I won't," she replied as she hugged him tighter.

And then they got up and had breakfast with Gabby, and she would forget about it until the next time it happened again.

TRAILBLAZERS

Cassie spent as much time with Reòll at the Pond House as possible. After her job at the inn, she would hitch a carriage ride to the restaurant. She often watched the children of the employees and was especially fond of Marion, the McIntires' daughter. She often took them for hikes and sometimes accompanied Thomas McIntire, locally known as the Trailblazer as well as the proprietor of the Jordan Pond House and an avid hiker. They took the children from the island villages with them. The kids vied for the privilege of placing a stone on a mountaintop cairn by clearing their section of a trail first. Mr. McIntire rewarded the children with popovers and homemade ice cream at the Jordan Pond House.

Cassie laughed as she thought about Gabriel. He always seemed to be first to the top of each mountain. It was great fun and quite an accomplishment. Cassie marveled that Thomas McIntire constructed a vast network of two hundred miles of trails on the island. Often, they would meet other people working on the paths. One person in particular was named Waldron Bates. He was known as the Path Maker.

Cassie knew that the trail system in and around the island evolved over centuries from Native Americans and rusticators, including Hudson River artists Thomas Cole and Frederic Church. Mr. Bates was chair of the Roads and Paths Committee of the Bar Harbor Village Improvement Association. He built stone stairways and iron rung ladders into trails with cliffs and other steep areas. She felt like these trails were part of her mission to improve access so that people could get to enjoy these wonderful places in the forests, mountains, and spectacular views from the summits.

One day working at the inn, she met a wonderful woman from Boston named Eliza Homans, who summered on Mount Desert Island. She met Cassie and always wanted to talk about the island, its beauty and fragility, and what she would do to help save it. She wanted more than anything to protect the island from exploitation and greed. Just in the last few years, she became the first donor of land, 140 acres on Beehive Mountain, including a glacial cirque known locally as the Bowl. It was the first donation to the Hancock County Trustees of Public Reservations and the second land trust in the whole nation.

Cassie passionately stated, "Mrs. Homans, it is an honor to meet you. Working here at the inn gives me such a special opportunity to meet famous people, especially those doing such good work. Thank you for your generosity and dedication and all you are doing for us and the future."

"You are welcome, my dear."

FINDING THE FUR

As time passed, their love for Seal Harbor and Mount Desert Island grew. The rusticators became more and more advocates for preserving this paradise for themselves and future generations.

With ever-increasing number of visitors coming to the island, the congregations of the new churches were growing. Reverend McDonald's church was in membership, and it was decided to put in a large pipe organ that would take anywhere between two and five years to install.

When Cassie heard this, she became worried that someone would discover the seal hide that she had hidden behind the choir loft in the church. She and Reòll were so happy together. She thought of all the myths and legends that surrounded selkies. If they found their skins and put them on, they would immediately return to the water world from whence they came and would never be able to return to their human existence. Now she knew that Reòll did not want to do that. She trusted him and decided it was time to have a conversation about the hide.

They sat together on a large rock and gazed out over Jordan Pond. The sun was setting, and the pink granite mountain sides glowed with the evening light. Cassie brought up the subject of the new pipe organ and suggested that they inspect the area where the organ would be built. Reòll agreed.

Cassie said, "Reòll, there is something I need to talk to you about. I trust you implicitly and know that you will not leave me, but I need you to know that at the time you came to me, I took your fur and hid it. What do you think of that?"

Reòll smiled and took her into his arms, kissing her forehead, and stated, "Cassie, you know I am telepathic and can read your thoughts. I have always known that. I know that my seal skin is hidden in the choir loft of the summer church. I think it is time that we retrieve it. I am sorry that you have worried about that all these years. You know I love you more than my life, and I live to protect you."

Cassie began to weep and held him as tight as she could. With a whimper, she cried, "Okay, we will go tomorrow morning and retrieve the hide."

Reòll whispered, "Eddie gave me that wonderful ash basket to carry it in. He did not say so directly but indicated that I needed the basket for something special. He is so wise."

The next day was sunny and hot, and they took the pack basket with them as they walked with Gabriel to the village.

"I love this church with its steeply-pitched gabled roof," exclaimed Cassie as they approached the entrance recessed behind a large stone arch. As they entered the vestibule, to the left, there was a doorway leading to a stairwell to the second-floor level that included the choir loft overlooking the main part of the church. Because of the stone structure, the church was cool, a blessing in the heat of August.

Cassie went quickly to the place in the eaves where she found the fur hide right where she left it. She retrieved it and held it to her chest, looking contemplatively at Reòll.

Gabriel looked puzzled. "Papa, what is that?"

Reòll replied, "That, my son, is something for you to ask questions about." And he patted his son on the head and hugged him. "It is a gift that I treasure and may come in handy someday. Feel how soft it is."

"Well! Why is it hidden here?"

"Your mama thought it would be safe in this sacred place, and she put it here for safekeeping. I will take care of it now." And he put it carefully in the basket where it would stay…for now.

They finished tidying up the rest of the sanctuary and sat in the front pew in silent prayer, gazing at the Communion table and cross. They were hungry. It was time for lunch, and it was a long walk home.

They walked out into the hot noonday sun and stopped to sit for a moment on the time rock and to look at the surf that was higher than normal on this beautiful day. They held hands and enjoyed being together as a family. Reòll stared at Bunker's Ledge and saw seals swimming far offshore. Gabriel watched the boats, some leisure, and some working crafts, bouncing in the harbor.

In a few moments, they continued on their way through the village and up the hill toward home. They didn't speak much. Holding hands all the way, they were grateful when they reached their house, where they felt safe and secure.

Gabriel had many questions, but it was apparent that the grown-ups didn't want to discuss anything right now. So he kept to himself, hoping that someday he would have answers.

THE OLDEST LAKE

Summer was drawing to an end. President Grover Cleveland, about fifteen years ago, signed a law making the first Monday in September a national holiday. Labor Day on Mount Desert Island was officially the end of summer, and the towns rolled up the streets and sidewalks, figuratively speaking, to await fall and give the locals a time to enjoy the most beautiful time of the year, bringing the changing of the color of the forest and trees, and of course, colder weather and the onset of winter and snow.

Cassie became more anxious and sometimes depressed every day and did not know why. *What is happening to me?* she lamented.

Reòll attempted to comfort her but to no avail.

They spent every possible moment together, loving, laughing, and enjoying their neighbors and the environment surrounding them. Reòll intensified his education, learning about humanity. He felt that it was his mission to be as human as possible and to experience as much humanity as he could, every minute. Each day he asked himself, *What have I learned? How can I make a difference? And can I teach my son these necessary lessons?*

They arose early this day in late August. The weather in the last few weeks was cooler. Fall always seemed to begin a little early here in Maine. If one was out and about in the evening, a sweater or light jacket was always called for.

This day was no different. Reòll packed sweaters and lunch in his pack basket, with his hide hidden under a false bottom in the basket. He, Cassie, and Gabriel planned on hiking on a trail on the other side of the pond and up the Jordan Mountain Cliff trail with ladders and rungs pounded into the rock face to assist the climb. They also took appropriate clothing to swim in the pond, even though it was known that most hikers to the lake, when there were no other people around, swam in what was called skinny-dipping, meaning without clothes. The lake was nestled in a little dip between the two mountain peaks, Green Mountain, and Sargent Mountain.

Called Sargent Mountain Pond, it was Maine's first lake, older than any other. It was the first lake to fill up with water as the glacier melted a hundred years before other lakes in Maine appeared. Sargent Mountain Pond sat alone in its granite bowl, among ancient pine trees, three hundred feet lower than the peak. It was 17,000 years old. At 1,373 feet, Sargent Mountain, named after the Sargent family who owned the land, was the second highest mountain on Mount Desert Island.

Reòll, Cassie, and Gabriel scampered up the cliff, along the narrow ledges, holding on to the metal rungs. The day was absolutely beautiful. They paused on a wide ledge with flaming blueberry foliage, turning color early this year. Finding a large rock to sit down, they sat for a while, gazing out over Jordan Pond toward the ocean and the islands beyond. The pond was rippling with a light wind, and the sky was slightly gray with puffy clouds hiding the sun that beamed through them in the early morning.

"This has to be the most beautiful spot on the island, maybe in the whole world," said Cassie.

Reòll agreed, happy that this was the place where he learned about being human.

Soon they continued on their way to the Penobscot peak and proceeded down into the dip between the mountains and on to the peaceful little lake resting between them. Gabriel had questions all the way, and Reòll attempted answers as best he could, fascinated that this was the oldest lake in Maine. They saw that no one was there but them, and they took off their clothes, placed them neatly on rocks, and waded into the ice-cold pond.

Reòll cautioned them not to swim out too far. He wasn't really worried about Gabriel because, with his webbed toes, he was a really good swimmer. But he was concerned about Cassie, knowing her fear of the water.

They paddled around a bit, enjoying the warm morning sun. Soon the chill of the water became too much, and they climbed out and donned their garments, glad to feel warm again.

They wanted to climb to the peak of Sargent Mountain, but with the clouds in the sky, they did not want to get caught in a possible rainstorm, so they decided to climb back down the way they came to the wide ledge where they had that beautiful view and where they could sit quietly and have the nice lunch that Reòll packed for them. After they finished eating, they ascended up to the peak of Penobscot Mountain, that was bare and rocky on top, with a gorgeous view and a trail across the top until it reached a gentler path that led back down to Jordan Pond that was not so steep and cliffy.

When they reached the Pond House, Reòll suggested that they sit on the porch and have tea and popovers since it was so close to the end of the season. That was the best treat one could imagine, and they enjoyed every bite and every minute, knowing that they would not have this opportunity again until next summer. They held hands across the rustic table and looked longingly into each other's eyes. Gabriel tolerated the lovey-dovey looks and giggled and, with his head bowed, looked away toward the mountains on the far side of the pond.

The End Is Near

They just finished their tea and popovers. It was late afternoon and a little chilly, but the day was still beautiful, and they were not ready to go home just yet. They would not have many more opportunities to enjoy this lovely spot, so they decided to walk back down to the pond and sit for a while on the lake shore.

They walked slowly through the meadow until they reached the path that encircled the pond. When they arrived at the shore, they found a wooden bench to sit upon, they snuggled together so they would all fit. There was a slight ripple on the pond from an evening breeze.

Reòll set the pack basket down beside them, leaned back against the back of the seat, and closed his eyes. He had a feeling in the pit of his stomach that caused him anxiety, another emotion that he experienced as a human. He wondered why, and he took a deep breath and decided to enjoy the moment. He loved his wife and son so much and was so grateful for this time of his being, knowing that it would not last forever, at least in this three-dimensional existence.

Cassie put her head on his shoulder and expressed her love for him. "Reòll! I don't know what I ever did without you in my life. I love you so much."

"Cassie, you have been my whole human existence. We were meant to be together. It was Divinely ordained. No matter what happens in the future, have faith that we will always be together with a connection that nothing in the universe can ever break. I love you too."

Gabriel was getting restless with all this love talk. He said, "I love you both. Can we go for a boat ride on the pond?" Eddie left his birch bark canoe on the dock that was recently built for the visitors to the pond house. "What do you think? I know he wouldn't mind if we paddled around a bit."

Cassie said, "That boat is one of his prize possessions. His uncle made it at their summer village. We will need to be very careful with it."

Reòll suggested that tonight was not a good time. The sky was a little cloudy off to the east. "Cassie! I think we should go home now. It's getting a little chilly, don't you think?"

"Oh, Reòll! I think it will be all right, and you did bring sweaters in case it got cold."

Reòll reluctantly retrieved the wraps out of the basket and handed them to Cassie, who helped Gabriel into his. Reòll stated emphatically, "You go ahead and be careful. I will wait here on the bench and watch you. Canoes can be difficult to maneuver if a wind arises, so you will need to be very careful. Please stay near the shore."

"We will! Don't worry." With that, the two scampered off toward the dock.

The boat was very light and slipped easily into the water. Cassie stood up carefully and held on to a piling on the pier and held her free hand out to help Gabriel into the boat. They both sat down, Cassie in the back, and Gabriel, facing her, sat in the front of the canoe. They both picked up a paddle and slipped easily out, just a little way from the shore, and swiftly swept down the pond.

Cassie closed her eyes to focus on the breeze blowing gently on her cheeks. *This is heaven,* she thought.

Reòll looked toward the bubble-shaped mountains, and the sky was a littler grayer with a very faint rainbow. His first thought was not "Oh, how beautiful!" His first thought was "*Oh no!* This is it."

Before any sign of a storm approaching, he walked quickly into the woods with his pack basket and found a spot where he would not be seen but could still see Cassie and Gabriel as they drifted out toward the center of the pond. His heart was heavy because he could sense what was about to occur. He unpacked his skin and held it tightly, and he wept.

He glanced toward the mountains and saw that the sky was becoming darker, and the wind was beginning to blow. He shouted to Cassie to come quickly ashore, but the wind was pushing the canoe farther and farther out. The more they paddled, the more the wind fought them, and steering the boat was completely impossible.

It came upon them suddenly—a microburst, almost like a tornado. The sky became like night. The wind picked the canoe up out of the water, and it came crashing down, throwing Cassie and Gabriel into the lake. Reòll heard Cassie scream as he quickly slipped into his seal hide. Gabriel was a good swimmer but could not reach his mother. He thrashed around but was helpless. The vortex caused by the raging wind began to pull them down, down, down. The pond was very deep, and they were entangled by the seaweed that was thrashing back and forth on the bottom.

Reòll slipped silently and unseen into the water and swam quickly to where Cassie was ensnarled by the bottom reeds. Gabriel was pulling at his mother as hard as he could but was beginning to lose consciousness. Reòll disentangled her and slipped under her so that she was resting on his back. He took hold of Gabriel's sweater and began swimming toward the surface. Soon, he had them back to the shore and swam to the dock where he could deposit his son and slid Cassie onto the deck. He took turns breathing into their mouths until they began breathing on their own. No one saw what transpired because they all took shelter from the terrifying storm.

Reòll stayed with his family, snuggling between them to keep them warm, and watched to see if anyone was coming. There was a lot of damage to the boats and dock, and soon, people from the Pond House became alarmed and began running down the path to the shore. At that time, he knew it was time to go before anyone saw him. He nuzzled Cassie and Gabriel, paused a moment to say goodbye, and slipped into the water, swimming toward the end of the pond that connected to Jordan Stream that connected to Little Long Pond and the ocean.

When the people from the Pond House got to the dock, Thomas and Nellie saw Cassie and Gabriel lying half-conscious. They were shocked, astonished, and very concerned. They called out, "Someone get some blankets and bring stretchers!" They hovered over the two with many questions. "What on earth happened, and where is Reòll?"

Cassie looked bewildered and didn't have any answers.

Gabriel awoke screaming, "Papa, Papa! Where is my papa?"

Rescuers came with stretchers and carried them back up the hill to the Pond House. Reòll was nowhere to be found.

REÒLL IS GOING HOME

Reòll swam to the end of the pond. His heart was broken. If seals could cry, he was weeping, his salt tears blending with the clear turbulent water of Jordan Pond. He leapt over the dam and into the rushing, overflowing steam. He was grateful for the flooded stream that would help him in his rush to the ocean.

As he reached Long Pond, it was easy for him to swim through the seawall barrier between the pond and the salty water of Bracy Cove. Soon, he was in open water that was fuming from the storm that had ended as fast as it had come and was well out to sea by now. He popped his head up out of the water and turned to look one last time to the place he called home for the last years. He paused and pondered all that he had known, learned, and loved. He fulfilled his mission. He knew that, but it did not make him feel any better as he thought about what he was leaving behind.

He turned and swam out to sea as he began to feel his sense of time return to the universal clock. He could sense his body dissolve into energy and rise above the ocean. He became invisible to the human eye and ascended quickly, thinking, *This must be how it feels for people when they die…*

Going from the glorious light of earth, immediately to the darkness of outer space. Even the stars disappeared. The experience would have been frightening if he didn't have memories emerging of the Source from whence he came. It all came rushing at him, his awareness of his Divine being. He looked back at the Earth, a pale-blue ball, ever so small and distant and gloriously beautiful. And he thought of all the humanity that lived there.

He thought, *My Cassie is there with my beloved son, Gabriel.* He thought of all the history and evolution that happened and was still happening on that little dot of light in the vastness of space, and he was overcome with wonder.

Now he thought about Cassie and his mission. *I did what I was sent to Earth to do. I took care of my family for over one hundred years. I know I will be reunited with Catherine when I get there.*

As far out into the cosmos he traveled, he could see a shiny golden cord, and he knew that the other end, though invisible, would be attached to Cassie's heart, and the connection would never, ever be broken. That gave him great comfort, though he knew she would grieve. Somewhere in her subconscious mind she would feel the connection, but that would not alleviate the pain and grief that she would feel. He was pained at the thought of her suffering, and all he could do was send his unconditional love through the golden cord and work from his dimension to help guide her to her destiny.

He thought about Gabriel. He knew he was special…born to do great things. Perhaps he would be able to guide him too.

Now everything was completely evolved. He was surrounded by the most beautiful lights that he ever experienced. They were like the aurora borealis on Earth, but so much more indescribable. He could see sparks of light surrounding him, and he knew they were individual souls from the Source welcoming him home, and he felt like they were all filling him with love. The white light at the Source was tinged with gold. It was brighter than the sun but not hot. It was warm and felt like love.

Everything seemed to be happening simultaneously. In this timeless state, all this had already happened. Prior to this, it was like he was living in a book, one page at a time. And now the book had completely ended, and he was experiencing it all at once in this exquisitely bright glow of the Divine. It was all light and love—nothing else.

Reòll was home.

EPILOGUE

Cassandra sat on a bench with Eddie Wing Eagle. They grieved together the loss and disappearance of Reòll. Cassie slowly began to remember what happened on Jordan Pond on that fateful day. She thought about her vision of drowning and knew that it had come to fruition and that the creature in her dream was Reòll. She knew that he sacrificed his humanity to save them and that returning to sealdom, he would never again return to be a person. He saved their lives, and she hoped and prayed that he returned to his Source safely.

She apologized to Eddie for almost wrecking his canoe.

He said, "It is fine. It only had a few places that needed mending, and besides, your safety is the only thing that matters. You didn't know there was going to be a storm like that. I'm so glad no one was seriously injured."

Eddie found the pack basket that Reòll left in the woods, and he asked Cassie if he could have it because it reminded him of Reòll. Of course, she was happy for him to have it back, especially since it carried the seal hide all that time when they both knew that it would be needed in time.

Gabriel would grow into a handsome man, remembering his father. Cassie would tell him about Reòll and where he came from. There were many stories that only Gabriel and Eddie would know. He would continue with the work that Reòll was dedicated to—saving the seals in the harbor and preserving the land for future generations. He would work diligently, helping those who wanted to create a national park in the future.

Eddie and James would continue to help Charles with the lighthouse, knowing how important it was in saving lives, not to mention all the past history of Foghorn and the visions and what the great light meant to their family.

Mary finally came to believe in Cassandra's gift of sight and admired her mystic daughter. They continued to live on their beautiful and productive farm, raising sheep, whose wool Mary spun into yarn. The clock moved slowly for them, and they enjoyed every minute.

Eddie and Cassie stayed close friends. He watched over her as he knew Reòll would expect him to do.

Cassie continued to live in their log cabin. She worked with the McIntires for years and also did all she could to see that Mount Desert Island was respected and preserved.

Everyone missed Reòll. Many myths arose around his existence, like the way he arrived and how he disappeared. Cassie did not share the truth with anyone except Eddie and Gabriel and, of course, her off-island family. It was a mystery that would never be solved.

Jean Marie Ivey on Jordan Cliffs above Jordan Pond, 1980.

ABOUT THE AUTHOR

Jean Marie Ivey moved to Maine with her family in 1966 to become part of the National Park Service family at Acadia National Park. Her family lived in the Rockefeller gatehouse at Jordan Pond. Thus began her love affair with Acadia National Park and Mount Desert Island and especially the village of Seal Harbor. As well as being a full-time mother of seven, Jean Marie pursued a part-time career in photography and freelance illustrating, coauthoring the book *Maine Paradise* with Russell D. Butcher, published by Viking Press in 1972. She worked at the Jackson Laboratory in Bar Harbor as a biomedical technologist for thirty-three years and is now devoting her time to writing and art. She painted the pictures in this book, especially for this story. She also has fourteen grandchildren and four great-grandchildren who fill her heart with joy. *Selkie* is the seventh book Jean Marie has published. All have been about living in Maine, her great love. This book is closer in her spirit and love of Seal Harbor than can be expressed in words. She adores these characters. A lot of personal history is included in this story.

Books published by Jean Marie Ivey:

Maine Paradise
Facts and Fancy: Acadia National Park and Mount Desert Island
Cassie's Dream
The Vine and the Cross
The Road to Bluebeard's Castle
Maine Wonderland: The Way It Was
Selkie in Seal Harbor

Printed in the USA
CPSIA information can be obtained
at www.ICGtesting.com
LVHW021941160824
788480LV00008B/95

9 798891 576278